Y
STR

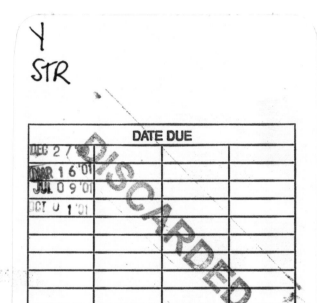

Strickland, Brad
Wishbone
Salty Dog #2

042099
y
STR

"I'm almost there," Sam called down to Joe and David.

Suddenly, the ladder she was climbing snapped right in two! David and Joe had to leap back as the whole thing collapsed.

"Sam!" David shouted.

Sam grabbed the edge of the loft and hung on. Slowly, painfully, she did a chin-up. Finally, she dragged herself all the way into the barn's loft.

"I'm okay, guys," Sam said.

The two boys let out a deep sigh of relief. "Hey, I smell something—smoke!" David yelled.

Sam looked down. The barn wall was glowing with fire. Thick, choking billows of gray smoke were pouring into the barn.

"Sam!" Joe yelled. "The barn's on fire! Hurry!"

The Adventures of **WISHBONE**™ titles in Large-Print Editions:

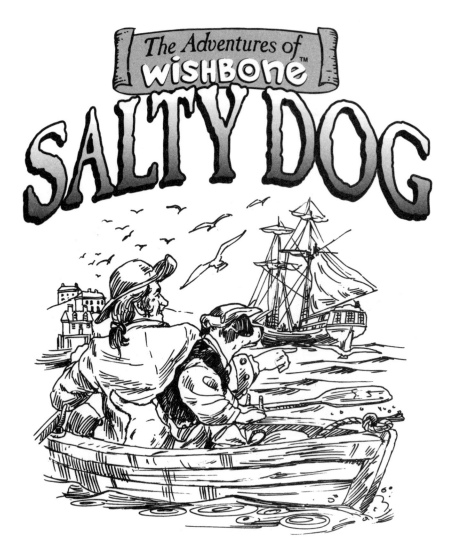

The Adventures of WISHBONE™
SALTY DOG

by Brad Strickland
Based on the teleplay by Mo Rocca
Inspired by *Treasure Island*
by Robert Louis Stevenson

WISHBONE™ created by Rick Duffield

Gareth Stevens Publishing
MILWAUKEE

This book is a work of fiction. The characters, incidents, and dialogues are products of the author's imagination and are not to be construed as real. Any resemblance to actual events or persons, living or dead, is entirely coincidental.

For a free color catalog describing Gareth Stevens' list of high-quality books and multimedia programs, call 1-800-542-2595 (USA) or 1-800-461-9120 (Canada). Gareth Stevens Publishing's Fax: (414) 225-0377.

Library of Congress Cataloging-in-Publication Data

Strickland, Brad.
    Salty dog / by Brad Strickland.
        p. cm.
    Originally published: Allen, Texas; Big Red Chair Books, © 1997.
    (The adventures of Wishbone; #2)
    Summary: When he accompanies Joe and his friends to look for treasure in the condemned Trumbull barn, Wishbone imagines himself as young Jim Hawkins who acquires a treasure map and soon finds himself involved with dangerous pirates.
    ISBN 0-8368-2298-6 (lib. bdg.)
    [1. Dogs—Fiction. 2. Buried treasure—Fiction. 3. Pirates—Fiction.
4. Adventure and adventurers—Fiction.] I. Duffield, Rick. II. Stevenson, Robert Louis, 1850-1894. Treasure Island. III. Title. IV. Series: Adventures of Wishbone; #2.
PZ7.S9166Sal   1999
[Fic]—dc21   98-47159

This edition first published in 1999 by
Gareth Stevens Publishing
1555 North RiverCenter Drive, Suite 201
Milwaukee, Wisconsin 53212 USA

© 1997 Big Feats! Entertainment. First published by Big Red Chair Books™, a Division of Lyrick Publishing™, 300 E. Bethany Drive, Allen, Texas 75002.

Edited by Kevin Ryan
Copy edited by Jonathon Brodman
Cover design and interior illustrations by Lyle Miller
Cover concept by Kathryn Yingling
Wishbone photograph by Carol Kaelson

Printed in the United States of America

1 2 3 4 5 6 7 8 9 03 02 01 00 99

To the great readers of
the Schaumburg Township schools

FROM THE BIG RED CHAIR...

Oh...hi! Wishbone here. You caught me right
in the middle of some of my favorite things—books.
Let me welcome you to my brand-new book series,
THE ADVENTURES OF WISHBONE. In each of these
books I have adventures with my friends in Oakdale and
imagine myself as a character in one of the greatest stories
of all time. In **SALTY DOG**, I imagine I'm a young boy
named Jim Hawkins from Robert Louis Stevenson's
adventure story **TREASURE ISLAND**—an exciting tale
about pirates on the high seas, and buried treasure.

You're in for a real treat, so pull up
a chair and a snack and enjoy reading!

Chapter One

Wishbone trotted happily along a trail that wound through green, piny-scented woods. The day was beautiful, the sun warm on his back, the earth springy beneath his paws. Eyes bright, head high, tail wagging, he felt ready for anything.

Yes, sir! the little white-with-brown-spots dog thought joyfully. *This is the way everything ought to be. One Jack Russell terrier, alone and brave, ready to face adventure! Only, where are you, adventure? Helllooo! I'm looking for you! Come on! I'm bold! I'm courageous! I'm— YIPE!*

Beep! Beepity-beep! Startled, Wishbone glanced behind him. A thin woman was riding a bike down the trail. She wobbled slightly as she moved one hand to honk the little plastic horn with all the energy Wishbone might have put into chasing a cat—or begging for a snack. It was Wishbone's next-door neighbor, Wanda Gilmore, wearing an enormous red hat, huge goggles that made her look as if she had a bug's face, and a flower-print pantsuit. Wishbone leaped out of her way. He got along with Wanda—usually. Of course, she was unreasonably fussy about his burying bones in her yard; it was a fussiness Wishbone thought was uncalled for. After all, Wanda had such nice, soft, welcoming dirt in her flowerbeds. . . .

Close behind Wanda came four others on bikes. First in line was Ellen Talbot, with whom Wishbone and his best friend, Joe, lived. Ellen was Joe's mom—and a wonderful cook.

Wishbone cocked his head at her in a doggie "hello." "Hi, Ellen! *Great* breakfast today! My compliments on the kibble." When Ellen pedaled past without speaking, Wishbone sighed. "Nobody listens to the dog."

Next came Samantha Kepler, a girl wearing a yellow jersey and a red bike helmet. Wishbone gave her a big doggie smile.

"Hi, Sam! Bet you're feeling adventurous, too!" Samantha, like Wishbone, had a vivid imagination—and a love for excitement. On the next bike was David Barnes, an energetic boy in a dark blue sweater and a blue safety helmet. Wishbone liked David, too. He was a genius at building things, and was quick to laugh.

Wishbone's tail began to wag joyfully, because last of all came his very best friend, Ellen's son, Joe, a smiling, brown-haired boy dressed in a striped shirt, royal blue biking shorts, and a white helmet. He pulled up, grinning, and said, "Hey, there, boy! You knew we'd catch up sooner or later. Let's go!" He pushed off again.

Wishbone paused a moment. "Be there in a sec-

8

ond, Joe. I'm checking for the scent of exciting exploits!" He took a deep sniff of the morning air, feeling as if he were one with nature. A rich history of the area came in through his sensitive nose. *Hmm. Lots of squirrels live around here, and rabbits, too,* Wishbone thought. But squirrels weren't the adventurous type. Sure, it was fun to play tag with them, but when a squirrel was "it," Wishbone just couldn't get the furry little creature to chase him back!

A faint, old smell puzzled the little dog for a moment, and then he finally recognized it. Horses had been somewhere nearby, and horses *could* mean excitement! Cowboys and explorers rode horses! The horses Wishbone smelled, however, hadn't been around for years and years. He sighed and hurried after his friends.

Where was he going to find adventure? It was hiding from him that day. There he was, a dog on the prowl for excitement, and nothing exciting was happening.

Up ahead the trail widened and opened out onto a clearing. Through the trees Wishbone glimpsed a moldering gray barn, an old building with a weather vane in the shape of a running horse on its roof. The bikers had all stopped and were staring at the place as Wishbone came loping into the clearing. Junk cluttered the weed-overgrown ground—a rusting, abandoned threshing machine, a skeletal, broken-down tractor with briars growing through it, and other odds and ends. Everything smelled ancient to Wishbone— that is, everything except the paint on a new wooden sign that had been nailed to a post:

9

THIS PROPERTY CONDEMNED
CITY OF OAKDALE ORDINANCE #143

"Ah, we have arrived!" Wanda announced dramatically, pushing her goggles up onto her forehead. She became very enthusiastic now and then about her hobbies. Among other passions, she was wild about growing petunias and roses. When she latched on to a new hobby, she was like a dog with a bone— so Wishbone could really respect her enthusiasm! She had recently decided that long, invigorating bike rides to explore Oakdale were both healthy and fun, and again Wishbone heartily agreed. *There's nothing as great as a good long run in the countryside,* he thought. *Unless, of course, it's a daring exploit— or food!*

Gesturing grandly as she held a folded map of Oakdale, Wanda said, "My friends, I give you the Trumbull barn!"

Samantha—or "Sam," for short—stared at the barn as if it were an enchanted castle. "It's beautiful! It looks just like the barn he described in *Blackbeard's Horseshoe.*" She looked back at the rest of her companions, her eyes sparkling, and explained, "That's my favorite Trumbull book."

Wanda put her arm around Sam's shoulder. "Oh, I love that book, too."

Wishbone grinned so widely his tongue hung out. "Books! One of *my* favorite hobbies! Oh, gang, I know the Trumbull books. Great stuff! Of course, they'd be better without the horses and with more dogs, but they're full of adventure—hey, that's right!

I'm *looking* for adventure. Excuse me while I see if I can sniff some out!"

Behind Sam and Wanda, Joe, David, and Ellen exchanged glances. At one time Mr. Trumbull had been a local celebrity, the author of a number of books about horses, but he had died years ago.

David asked, "Did you ever read any of those books?"

Joe shook his head, but his mom, who was a librarian, nodded. "I've read them all. They're good," Ellen Talbot said. "You should read one sometime. You'd probably like it. I think Wanda and Samantha must be about the two biggest Trumbull fans around."

"What was the title you mentioned?" David asked Sam. *"Blackberry's Shoes?"*

"No, *Blackbeard's Horseshoe,*" Sam said impatiently. "Blackbeard was this fabulous black-and-white stallion."

"You know," Wanda said over her shoulder, "Mr. Trumbull really did have a horse named Blackbeard. Why, rumor has it that after Blackbeard died, Mr. Trumbull nailed his horseshoe somewhere into the walls of this barn."

Sam gave her a quick look. "Are you serious?"

Joe called out, "What's so special about this horseshoe?"

Sam shrugged and said, "Well, in the book, whoever owns the horseshoe has the courage to go anywhere, no matter what the risk."

Wishbone's tail wagged. "To boldly go where no dog has gone before! Yep, I could live with that! Sounds thrilling to me!"

With a determined nod, Wanda added, "To be a true explorer!" She sighed. "It's a shame the barn's being torn down."

Sam's expression became sad. "Oh, Ms. Gilmore, I have to go get inside that barn before it's gone! I need to find Blackbeard's horseshoe."

Ellen said kindly, "But that's impossible, Samantha. The barn's condemned. It's rickety and dangerous."

"That's right," Wanda agreed. She sighed again. "I just wanted you to see it before it's gone. Well, let's move on!" She held up her map, waving everyone back onto the trail.

With her eyes on the fluttering paper, Sam asked, "Can I have that?"

Wanda blinked in surprise. "The map? Well, of course." She handed it to Sam. Folded, it was the size of a tall, thin book. Its cover showed a red sun rising over the city skyline of Oakdale.

Sam took the map as if it were a golden treasure. "Thanks," she said. "I just want it as a souvenir."

Wanda nodded in an understanding way, then bellowed like a drill sergeant, "Let's go, people!"

Wanda, Ellen, David, and Joe moved off, pedaling their way down the trail. But Sam lingered behind. She unfolded the map and looked just south of the airport at the spot that Wanda had circled. It was the site of the old Trumbull horse farm—the very place where she now stood. She gazed at the map and then back at the barn, her eyes shining with anticipation.

Wishbone looked up at her. "Sam? Helllooo! What are you waiting for?"

12

Softly, as if speaking to herself, Sam said, "I'll be back, Blackbeard. I'll be back." Then she hopped onto her bike and rode away, leaving behind a very thoughtful Wishbone.

Hmm—do I feel an adventure coming on at last? Let's see: Sam's curious, and she's courageous, and she's a kid. Oh, yes! That DEFINITELY spells adventure. It also spells the name of one of my favorite books, written by the Scottish author Robert Louis Stevenson in 1883. It's a story of danger on the high seas and a hidden treasure in a far-away place. The story begins on the southwest coast of England at a place called the Admiral Benbow Inn, and it's about a brave and smart young lad named Jim Hawkins.

And the title of the story? Why, matey, it's one that always sends a shiver of excitement from my nose right down my spine to the tip of my tail, or from stem to stern, as you might say. The title is . . . *TREASURE ISLAND!*

Chapter Two

So Wishbone imagined himself as an English boy living near a little seaside village named Black Hill Cove in the 1760s. He could see the ocean sparkling in the morning sunlight. He could also imagine the cobblestone road leading out of the village. It snaked up the steep hill, past a great stone house—named the Hall—where the important local landowner, Mr. Trelawney, lived. The road crossed a bridge and wound still higher. At the top of the hill stood a gray stone inn, two stories tall. It had a steep black-slate roof, and over the front door was a colorful red-and-blue sign with a painting of a British admiral on it. The sign read: ADMIRAL BENBOW INN. Wishbone imagined that he was Jim Hawkins, the boy who told the story. . . .

Yes, folks, this is my home, the Admiral Benbow Inn! It's a wonderful place, with benches in front of big sunny windows where I can curl up and tuck my tail over my nose for a nap on cold winter days.

There are cool nooks and crannies under the stairs where I can snooze when it's hot in the summer. Here, in this comfortable inn, I live with my father and mother.

I remember the brown, old sailor as if it were yesterday. He came plodding to the front of the inn, pulling his sea-chest behind him in a handbarrow. He was tall and strong. Running across one of his cheeks was the scar from a saber cut. He looked around, and then in a high, cracked voice he began to sing an old sea-song:

Fifteen men on the dead man's chest—
Yo-ho-ho, and a bottle of rum!

He rapped on the door. When my father let him in, he called roughly for a glass of rum. Before my father—who was very ill—could bring it, the old sailor snatched a glass from another customer and downed the drink in a gulp.

I blinked at this rudeness and thought, *O-kay. Self-service is fine, if that's what you want.*

When he had finished his drink, he growled, "This is a handy cove. Much company, mate?"

My father told him no, we had very little company.

"Well, then," said he, "this is the place for me. I'm a plain man; rum and bacon and eggs is what I want, and that cliff up there for watching ships. Call me captain—there!" He threw down three or four gold pieces. "Tell me when that runs out!"

I trotted upstairs ahead of him to show him where to put his heavy sea-chest. He followed me into a front room, and I grabbed the curtains in my teeth and opened them to show him how his window looked out over the cliffs to the great blue ocean. He grunted in satisfaction and then asked what my name was.

"Jim!" said he when I told it to him. "Look here." He held out a silver fourpenny piece. "Would ye like to have that?"

"Yes, sir," I said. That was more money than I usually had in *two* months. I could use it to buy a new squeaky toy! Maybe two!

The captain grinned. "All right, matey. Be my lookout. Keep a sharp eye open for . . ."—he turned pale and swallowed hard—". . . for a seafaring man with one leg," he croaked. "And tell me double quick if ye see him.

16

Keep watch, and I'll give ye a silver fourpenny piece every month, regular as a clock!"

I nodded enthusiastically and thought, *Sounds like a deal to me! Just call me hawkeye Hawkins! I'll be the best lookout who ever looked an out!*

Every month after that he paid me my fourpenny piece, though no one-legged sailor ever appeared. But the captain seemed so frightened just talking about the one-legged man that I became afraid, too. I remember a terrible dream I had one night when the wind shook the house and the surf roared along the cove and surged up the cliffs.

In my dream, I took the doorknob in my teeth and opened the door to empty the bucket of water I had used to scrub the floor. I heard a sound coming from the bridge, and my ears perked up. What I saw made my fur stand on end and stopped me dead on my paws. A monstrous creature, ten feet tall, with huge claws and a mouth full of razor-sharp teeth, was bounding up the hill toward me. He was dressed like a sailor. He had only one leg, which grew from the middle of his body, and he sprang along on this bizarre limb in huge leaps. I ran, pumping my four legs as hard as I could, but he jumped after me, coming closer and closer. I felt his hot breath on the fur covering the back of my neck—and I woke up shivering from nose to tail.

I like a game of chase as much as the next guy, but this is too scary for young Jim Hawkins! I wanted ADVENTURE, not a horror show!

Our new guest stayed on for months. Autumn transformed itself into a sharp, cold winter, but his habits never changed. I stayed inside to keep the frost out of my fur, but the captain went for a long walk every day to stare at the ships through a brass telescope. At night he sat and drank rum-and-water very strong. And guess who had to wear his poor little front paws to the bone scrubbing up everything after he spilled it? Uh-huh. Some adventure! Jim Hawkins, professional mop artist!

When the captain had had too much rum, he would roar and bellow and thump the table, and he would force folks to accompany him in singing his old sea-songs. He scared people with his stories—dreadful tales about hanging, and walking the plank, and storms at sea, and wild deeds, and places on the Spanish Main. My sick father was always saying customers would stop coming and the inn would be ruined financially. But people liked the excitement of those hair-raising stories, and they came to hear them night after night; they called the captain a real British sea-dog.

In one way the captain did hurt the inn, for after my poor father took to his bed and could no longer get about, my mother was afraid to ask the captain for more money. He went on living at the inn until he owed us a large sum.

Toward the end of my father's life, a disturbing event took place. The local physician, Dr. Livesey, came late one afternoon to visit his patient, and afterward he ate dinner at the inn. The doctor was a neat, quick man, with a powdered wig as white as snow, bright, black eyes, and a pleasant manner. After dinner, he called me over to where he sat in the parlor. "Jim," the doctor began kindly, "you know your father is very ill."

I looked down, my heart feeling heavy, my tail drooping toward the floor. "Yes, sir, but he'll get better, won't he?"

The doctor patted the fur on my shoulders gently. "I'm afraid not, Jim. He's worn out and suffering. And he's worried that soon he'll be gone, and you'll be the man of the house. He wanted me to tell you to look after your mother when he's no longer here."

I couldn't answer, for I was crying.

Just then, from his table across the room, the captain piped up his eternal song:

Fifteen men on the dead man's chest—
Yo-ho-ho and a bottle of rum!
Drink and the devil had done for the rest—
Yo-ho-ho and a bottle of rum!

Dr. Livesey looked up, annoyance on his face, upon hearing the loud, grating voice. Everyone else fell silent, but Dr. Livesey went on talking. "Jim," he said, "I know how hard it is when—"

The captain glared at him, slapped the table, and shouted, "Silence between decks!"

Some people are like that. No matter how bad you feel, they bark at you for no reason at all.

Coldly, the doctor turned to him and said, "I have only one thing to say to you, sir, and that is if you keep on drinking rum, the world will soon be rid of a very dirty scoundrel!"

The captain's face grew red. He sprang up, drew a sailor's knife from his belt, and threatened, "I'll pin ye to the wall, ye swab!"

The doctor's voice was calm and steady. "There is a sick man upstairs who does not need your noise. If you do not put that knife away, I promise, on my honor, you shall hang."

The captain looked uncertain. He muttered something, put down the knife, and sat down, grumbling.

"Now, sir," Dr. Livesey continued, "I shall keep an eye on you. If you cause any complaint, I'll have you arrested!"

The captain did not answer. He kept quiet the rest of that evening, and for the remainder of the week.

Then one cold January morning an evil-looking sailor, a pale, scrawny man missing two fingers from his left hand, came asking for the captain, but our guest was out looking at ships. This suspicious-looking ruffian made the fur on my shoulders bristle and I didn't trust him. Mother was upstairs with my father, and the gruff stranger forced me to wait for the captain until he—the sailor referred to the captain as "my old shipmate Bill"—returned.

When the captain came through the doorway, the stranger made his voice loud and bold as he shouted, "Bill!"

The captain looked as if he had seen a ghost, and I felt sorry to see him turn so old and sick. "Black Dog!" he gasped.

I blinked in surprise and thought, *I must have been mistaken! With a name like that, he's got to be a good guy. Doesn't he?*

20

"Aye, Black Dog as ever was, come for to see his old friend Billy Bones," the stranger replied. "Now we'll sit down, if ye please, and talk square, like old shipmates."

I began to scrub the floor, working the brush slowly with my paw. For a long time they argued in voices so low that even I—with my excellent hearing—couldn't make out what they were saying.

At last, the captain cried out, "No, no, no! If it comes to swinging, swing all, say I." Then all of a sudden the chair and table clattered to the floor, a clash of steel followed, and the next instant I saw Black Dog running away and the captain pursuing him with drawn sword, slashing it in the air. Just at the door, the captain aimed one last tremendous cut, which would have killed Black Dog if it had struck him. But the sword caught on the inn's big wooden signboard.

I barked out, "Hey, hey, hey! Captain, that's going to have to come out of your damage deposit!" But the captain was cursing so loudly that he didn't seem to hear me.

Black Dog ran for his life down the road. The captain stood staring at the signboard. At last he turned around and came back inside.

"Jim," said he, "rum." As he spoke, he almost fell.

"Are you hurt?" cried I.

He shook his head. "Rum! I must get away from here. Rum!"

As I hurried to get it, a loud crash came from the parlor. I ran back, my nails clicking on the wooden floor, and found the captain lying stretched out unconscious. Just then Mother hurried downstairs to

21

see what the noise had been about. Between us we raised the captain's head. He was breathing loudly and hard, and his face was a horrible bluish color.

Mother cried, "What a disgrace! And with your poor father sick!"

Neither of us knew what to do, and we were relieved when the door opened and Dr. Livesey came in, on his visit to my father.

"Doctor!" I said. "There's been a fight. He's wounded!"

"Wounded? Fiddlesticks! He's had a stroke, just as I warned him. Mrs. Hawkins, you run upstairs to your husband and tell him nothing. I'll try to save this rascal's life. Jim, get me a basin."

When I brought it, I saw the doctor had ripped the captain's sleeve. The old sailor's arm was tattooed: "Here's Luck," "Fair Wind," and "Billy Bones His Fancy" were all neatly marked on his forearm. "Thank you, Jim," the doctor said when he took the basin from my mouth. "And now, Master Billy Bones—if that is your name—we'll have a look at your blood. Are you afraid of blood, Jim?"

"N-no, sir," I said. "N-not very much. B-but I don't like the smell of it."

Yow! Doctors used to treat patients by "bleeding" them. They would use a sharp little scalpel that looked like a miniature shovel. It was called a lancet. Holding it with great care, they sliced into an arm vein, and they would collect a pint or so of blood in a basin. They thought this process removed poison, and—and if you don't mind, I'll just look the other way for a while. . . .

23

"Here, Jim, hold the basin," said Dr. Livesey. He bled the captain, and a long time passed before the doctor bandaged up the man's arm and took the basin from me.

When I looked back around, the old sailor opened his eyes and blinked. He tried to raise himself, crying, "Where's Black Dog?"

"There's no Black Dog here," the doctor said. "You have been drinking rum and have had a stroke, just as I told you. Now, Mr. Bones, one glass of rum won't kill you, but if you take one you'll take another and another, and if you drink rum, you'll die! Do you understand? Come, and I'll help you to bed."

With much trouble we got him upstairs to his bed, where his head fell back on the pillow.

"Come with me, Jim," the doctor said. As soon as he had closed the door, he told me, "I have drawn enough blood to keep him quiet for a while. The best thing is for him to lie where he is for a week. No rum for him. Another stroke will kill him."

Understood, Doctor! But then later, the captain asked for rum. I explained what the doctor had said. He didn't agree.

The captain muttered, "Doctors is all swabs. Look, Jim, how my fingers fidges. I'll have the horrors. I seen old Flint in the corner behind you, plain as print."

"Flint? Who is Flint?"

"Who *was* Flint, matey. He was a pirate, and a murderous one. But I won't imagine him standing there if I has a little rum. The doctor said one glass wouldn't hurt me. I'll give you a gold piece for a drink, Jim."

No matter how many rubber bones a gold piece might buy, I didn't want his money. But at last, to keep him quiet, I gave him one very small glass of rum. He drank it greedily and then said he had to be off. He was too weak to move, and at last he growled, "Thunder! That doctor's done me." After a moment, he added, "If I can't get away and they tip me the black spot, they're after my sea-chest. Jim, if they give me the black spot, you run to this doctor swab and tell him to pipe all hands, and he'll find Flint's crew here at the Admiral Benbow."

"The black spot?" I asked. "What's that?" I once knew a Spot, but he was white-and-gray. Nice guy, for a bulldog.

"That's a summons," the captain explained. "They draw a black spot on a piece of paper and hand it to me. It means the crew is going to turn against me. They want what's mine. I was old Flint's first mate, and I'm the only one as knows the place. He gave the map to me in Savannah when he lay dying. But don't you go unless they put the black spot on me, or unless you see the seafaring man with one leg, Jim!"

I didn't say it, but I thought, *A little hung up on one-legged sailors, aren't we, Captain?*

He fell asleep after that. I don't know what I would have done if things had gone well, but that very evening my mother came downstairs weeping. My heart sank.

"Is—is Father—?" I began to ask.

"Oh, Jim, he's gone," she said, her voice breaking into a sob. She hugged me. "We've got to be brave, Jim."

25

"Yes, Mother," I said miserably. I felt terrible. I wanted to creep into a dark corner, howl, put my head down on my paws, and never come out again.

It was an awful time. With our sorrow, the arranging of the funeral, and the daily work to be done at the inn, I didn't have time to think of the captain's troubles. Over the next few days he got somewhat better. He limped downstairs to eat his meals, but he talked very little. He seemed lost in his own thoughts.

Then, a few weeks after my father's funeral, there came tapping along the high road a second stranger, a ragged old beggar with a green cloth bound over his eyes. He cried out, "Will any kind friend inform a poor blind man where he may be?"

"You're at the Admiral Benbow Inn at Black Hill Cove," said I.

"I hear a voice," said he. "A young voice. Will you take my hand, my kind young friend, and lead me in?"

I held out my paw, and the horrible creature gripped it like a vise. "Now, you boy," he said, "take me in to the captain, or I'll break it."

"Ouch!" I cried. "Hey, watch it!" Grrr—if this guy had been a cat, I would have shown him a thing or two! Now I could smell familiar scents: salt, tar, and that sour combination of anger and fear that was the same as Black Dog's smell—and, come to think of it, much like the captain's, too.

The stranger twisted my paw so painfully that I led him to where our sick old buccaneer was sitting.

"Here he is," I said with a gasp.

"Bill!" the blind man screeched. "Here's an old friend!"

The poor captain's face turned pale with horror. He croaked, "Blind Pew!"

"Sit where you are, Bill," the beggar said. "If I can't see, I can hear a finger stirring. Hold out your left hand. Boy, take his left hand by the wrist, and bring it near to my right." I saw him pass something into the captain's hand. The blind man then turned and rushed out.

The captain stared at the piece of paper in his hand. "The black spot!" he cried. "They give me until ten o'clock. Six hours. We'll do 'em yet, Jim!" He leaped to his feet, swayed, then fell straight to the floor. I ran for my mother, but we were too late. The captain had been struck dead by a thundering stroke, as the doctor had warned.

I told my mother what had happened, and she said, "The captain owed us money, and these ship-mates of his will certainly not leave us a penny. We'll have to take it ourselves."

I stared at her. Was she crazy? I had just told her that Pew and his shipmates were coming! But my mother never changed her mind about anything—not even when I gave her all sorts of reasons why I didn't *need* a bath. So I crouched beside the captain's body and pawed at his pockets, searching for the key to his sea-chest. I found only his knife, a few coins, a thimble, some thread, and some big needles.

"Perhaps the key's around his neck," my mother suggested.

Clever! I should have thought of checking his collar! And there, sure enough, was the key, hanging from a string. Grabbing it in my teeth, I yanked it free and gave it to Mother. We hurried upstairs to his room. His sea-chest was old and battered, with the initial "B" burned into the top. My mother unlocked it, releasing a strong smell of tobacco and tar. Whew! The captain could have used a soup bone and liver air freshener!

We found a suit of good clothes, four pistols, a piece of bar silver, an old Spanish watch, a pair of brass-mounted compasses, and five West Indian seashells. Then came an old boat cloak, and below that a bundle tied up in oilcloth, looking like papers, and a canvas bag jingling with coins.

"I'm an honest woman," my mother said. "I'll take no more than he owed us."

"Uh, Mom? Helllooo! With pirates lurking nearby, I'd suggest we simplify our plan. Grab everything and run, run, run!" I said. But she insisted on taking only the exact amount. The task required more than two hours' work. Counting was hard because the coins were of all countries and sizes. There were doubloons, louis-d'ors, guineas, pieces of eight, and I don't know what else. Mother would take only English money. As she was counting, my ears suddenly pricked up. I heard the tap-tapping of the blind man's stick on the frozen road. "The pirates are early! They're here!" I yelped.

Mother jumped to her feet. "This much will have to do."

I grabbed the oilcloth pouch in my mouth. "I'll take this to make it even," I mumbled.

We hurried downstairs and slipped out the side door, and not a second too soon, for I heard voices around at the front. It was a freezing night. We ran in the shadows until we reached the bridge that led over the river and into the village. Not daring to cross it in full view of the inn, we slipped down the bank on all fours—which was harder for my mother than for me. Then we hid, lying on our stomachs in the frosty grass. By the way, if you've never tried it, it's not very comfortable. Stomach fur is too thin to keep the chill out!

I peeked back to see what the villains were doing. Six or seven men stood outside the inn, and one shouted, "Down with the door!" I shivered. The voice was that of the blind Mr. Pew.

"Aye, aye, sir!" answered two or three, but they found the door unlocked.

The blind man ordered them inside, and after a moment someone called out, "Bill's dead!"

"Search him, you lubbers! Then go aloft and find the chest!" Pew ordered them.

Within seconds someone threw open the captain's window and yelled, "Pew, they've turned out the chest alow and aloft!"

"Is Flint's map there?" Pew bellowed.

"We don't see it."

At that, Pew cursed like a madman. "It's the people of the inn. If I had that boy here, I'd put his eyes out! Maybe they're close by. Scatter and search!"

Uh—excuse me? Could I change my order from adventure to a plain dog biscuit? No? I was afraid of that!

Just as the men came outside, we heard a whistle from the other side of the bridge. "There's the lookout!" one of the men shouted. "We'll have to run!"

29

"Run! No!" Pew screamed. "Oh, shiver my soul, if I had eyes!" And he began to strike about him with his stick.

The whistle came again, sharper than before, and then a pistol shot rang out. That was clearly a signal of danger from their lookout, for all the buccaneers ran in every direction. They left Pew behind, stumbling and groping.

"Shipmates!" Pew cried in fear. "Johnny, Black Dog, don't leave old Pew!"

Just then I heard and smelled horses, and four or five riders galloped across the bridge. Pew screamed, ran across the road, and fell into a ditch. He scrambled up again, but he was bewildered and dashed right under the horses. I heard a horse neigh as Pew screeched in fear. He fell under the hooves. The leaping horses couldn't help trampling him. He tumbled from beneath their hooves like a bundle of old clothes. Pew rolled on his side, then gently collapsed on his face. He did not move again. Blind Pew was stone dead.

Ahoy, mates! 'Tis I, Wishbone. Perhaps ye may be all at sea because o' the pirate talk. Well, here's
Wishbone's Pirate-to-English Dictionary.
This will explain some of the unusual expressions the pirates use.

ahoy!:   a seafaring person's way of saying "hi!" When two ships come alongside each other, one captain will call out "Ahoy!" to the captain of the other vessel.

avast!:   a command used to warn someone to "Watch out!" or "Get away!"

bow: the front part of a ship.

doubloon: an old Spanish gold coin.

gentleman of fortune: a pirate.

gig: a small boat that will hold five or six people.

jolly-boat: a large boat that can either be rowed with oars or used with a sail.

lay to: to bet on something.

lubber: a clumsy fellow. In a sailor's world, anyone who does not know how to raise a sail or steer a course is a lubber!

maroon: to abandon someone and put him or her ashore alone on an island, left to try to get along as best as possible.

mate:	a friend. When someone is called "matey," it means he or she is a close friend and shipmate.
mutiny:	sailors take over a ship by using force and get rid of the officers in charge.
piece of eight:	an old Spanish silver coin.
pound sterling:	the main unit of British money (just as the dollar is the main form of American currency). British money was made up of many different units at the time *Treasure Island* was written, and everything was based on the pound sterling. The pound was broken down into shillings, pence, and farthings (just as the American dollar is divided into quarters, dimes, nickels, and pennies). A guinea was a little more than one pound. A pirate treasure of 700,000 pounds would have been worth millions of dollars in today's money. Just think of all the diamond-studded collars and high-rise doghouses that could buy!
quartermaster:	a subordinate officer of a ship who takes care of mechanical and maintenance details.
stern:	the rear portion of a ship.

Chapter Three

The others had run away like rabbits. Mother and I crept out of our hiding place and discovered that the riders were revenue agents out looking for smugglers. Their leader, Mr. Dance, said he had to report to Mr. Trelawney, our local judge, and asked me to come along. I trotted along beside him, up to the great house. In England, a squire is a rich man who owns a large estate of land, and our Mr. Trelawney was both rich and a land-owner, so we all called him Squire Trelawney out of respect. When we got there, we found that Dr. Livesey had come to have dinner. Squire Trelawney graciously invited us to eat before telling our story. Yum! Pass the chicken, pass the beef, pass the potatoes, pass the gravy, pass the kibble.

When we had finished our meal, Squire Trelawney and Dr. Livesey listened to Mr. Dance's report. When Mr. Dance finished his account, the squire, a tall, strongly built, red-faced man, said, "Mr. Dance, you are a noble fellow. As for riding down that villain, I hold you blameless. It was an accident, and he was a dog, sir!"

I thought, *Hmm . . . I'm beginning to see a pattern here. Maybe I should tell the squire that dogs aren't all bad.*

When Mr. Dance left, Dr. Livesey wanted me to tell my story. Both men listened to it with keen interest. "Jim," the doctor said, "do you have this thing they were looking for?"

"Here it is, sir," I replied. I had dropped the packet on the floor under the table. I jumped down from my chair and fetched it for him.

"Squire," Dr. Livesey said, taking the packet from my mouth, "have you heard of this Flint?"

"Heard of him!" the squire cried, sounding as excited as a pointer visiting a quail farm. "He was the most bloodthirsty buccaneer who ever sailed the seas! And his treasure is supposed to be greater than Blackbeard's! Blackbeard was a child compared to him! He was the terror of the Spanish! He was—"

"Come, Squire," interrupted the doctor. "You are so confoundedly hot-headed that I cannot get a word in. If this packet contains a clue to where Flint buried his treasure, will the treasure amount to much?"

"Amount, sir!" the squire shot back. "It will amount to this: I will fit out a ship and take you and Hawkins along, and we'll have that treasure if we have to search a year!"

What? Treasure! Now, if this isn't adventure, I wouldn't know it if I smelled it!

"Very well," the doctor said. "Now, if Jim agrees, I will open this packet."

If I agreed? This was Adventure with a capital A! Open, open, open! "Yes, Doctor," I told him, my tail wagging, "please do."

The bundle contained a book and a sealed envelope. The book's first page held the name "Mr. W. Bones, Mate." After that came columns of figures, sums of money, and other numbers.

"This is an account book," the squire observed. "Every time the pirates captured a ship, Mr. Bones recorded the nautical position and his share of the loot. Now for the other."

The doctor opened the sealed paper packet, and out fell a map of an island, with latitude and longitude, soundings, and names of hills, bays, and inlets. The men spread it open, and I held down a corner with my paw, staring at the chart as if it were a fresh, raw T-bone steak. The island was about nine miles long and five across, shaped like a fat dragon standing up. I saw hills and woods, a small fort, and three crosses marked in red ink. Beside one of them was the note, "Bulk of treasure here." Another read, "Bar silver here." The third was labeled "Arms." Directions for finding the hidden riches were scrawled on the back of the map. At the bottom, Mr. Bones had written that the map had been given to him in Savannah by Mr. J. Flint in the year 1754—seven years ago, for last month we had celebrated New Year's Day for 1761.

You know, that's a great idea that Captain Flint had. Remind me to make a map the next time I bury a bone in Wanda's yard!

The squire was delighted. "Livesey, find another doctor to care for your patients. I'll go to Bristol and buy a ship. In three weeks—two weeks—ten days— we'll have the best ship in England! We'll sail to this treasure island and return rich as lords!"

36

"Trelawney," the doctor replied, "I will go, but I am afraid of one man."

The squire's face grew bright red. "Who? Name the dog!"

I thought the squire was getting personal! I wished he would refer to bad people as cats!

"You!" the doctor exclaimed. "For you cannot hold your tongue. The men who attacked the inn tonight are desperate. If they should get wind of the fact that we have this map, they could become dangerous. You must not blab it about."

"Livesey," the squire responded, "you are right. I will be as silent as the grave."

The squire went to Bristol the next morning. A few weeks later, he sent a letter saying all was ready, and the doctor and I rode down in a speedy post-coach drawn by four sturdy horses. It was a good trip. I got to stick my head out the window with my tongue hanging out the whole way!

The moment we arrived and stepped out of the coach, the squire was there standing before us, dressed as a ship's officer and beaming all over his red face. He told us that he had bought a schooner called the *Hispaniola*. He had hired an experienced captain named Smollett and a cook named Long John Silver, an old navy man who had been badly wounded in battle. Silver now kept a tavern called the Spy-Glass, but he longed to be back again at sea. "He's a good man, sir!" Squire Trelawney said enthusiastically. "He knows all of the sailors, and he helped me put together a fine crew."

We walked near the waterfront. I was delighted to see ships of all nations. There were men who sang on deck while they worked, and others toiled high up in the rigging, like spiders crawling in their webs. I saw colorful figureheads, foreign flags, and sailors with rings in their ears, curly whiskers, and long pigtails. I took a deep breath and smelled tar! Salt! Adventure! The experience was wonderful.

"Now, Jim," the squire told me, "I want you to run straight down this street until you see the Spy-Glass tavern. Nip inside and tell Mr. Silver we're ready for him, and then you and he shall come aboard!"

I scampered along on my errand as fast as my four legs could carry me. Before long I nosed out the place, a bright little tavern with a newly painted sign, red curtains, and a clean, sanded floor. I looked inside and saw a crowd of seafaring men. A moment later, a man came out of a side room, and I knew he must be Long John. I ran up to him, saying, "Mr. Silver, sir?"

He turned to me with a wide smile. "Yes, lad, such be my name."

His leg! He had only one leg! Captain Billy Bones had warned me about a seafaring man with *one leg!* I whimpered in surprise.

"What is it, lad?" he asked, as I stared at him in horror. His left leg was cut off close to the hip, and he leaned on a wooden crutch.

"You—you have only one leg—" I blurted out before I knew what I was saying.

"What!" Silver shouted as he spun on his heel.

"Thunder! Which of ye swabs took my leg? Nobody leaves this here tavern until I finds the thief that stole my leg! I'll— Hang on a minute!" He turned back to me and winked. "Come to think of it, matey, that leg was took off by a cannon ball twelve leagues south-southeast o' Panama twenty years ago! Probably a little late to look for it, don't ye think?" He threw back his head and laughed.

Everyone joined in. I was embarrassed, but I could not help grinning. Long John's sense of humor startled me, but it made me want to laugh along. "I— I'm sorry," I stammered.

He clapped a huge hand on my back. "Don't worry, lad. I lost that timber in the service of the king, God bless him!"

"God bless King George!" shouted a dozen or so of the men, lifting their glasses.

"Now, what's your errand?" Silver asked, patting me on the head, right between my ears. My suspicions vanished. And why not? I thought I knew what pirates were like—ugly, dirty, low-down, raggedy men who smelled angry and fearful. But they were nothing like Long John, who was tall, with blond hair and a big, beefy, handsome face that was intelligent-looking, and cheerful. He might have been a sturdy English bulldog. And he was a cook, so he smelled like steak-and-kidney pudding, bangers-and-mash, bubble-and-squeak, and toad-in-the-hole—all delicious English dishes!

"Sir," I said, sitting near his foot, with my tail beginning to thump the floor, "I'm to tell you to report to the *Hispaniola* immediately."

He laughed once more. "So you're our cabin boy,

Jim Hawkins!" He leaned down and shook my paw with a firm grasp. "You're going to be a famous cabin boy, Jim. You're smart—smart as paint. I can see that right off!"

A delightful fellow, this Long John Silver! So perceptive! We walked along the quay, the salt-bleached wood warm under my paws, and Silver told me about all the ships. He was one of the friendliest men I had ever met, and I was sure he would be a fine shipmate.

At the waterside, he pointed across the harbor. "There she lies, Jim, the *Hispaniola*. A fine craft, is she not?"

I thought the *Hispaniola* was the most beautiful vessel in the harbor. She was a sleek schooner with two tall masts, shining white canvas sails spread fore and aft on them. Some men bustled on her deck, and others climbed in her rigging. She looked like a sleek bird ready to fly! Long John rowed us out to her. As soon as I came aboard, I reported to the cabin, where the squire and the doctor were. I found them having an argument with Captain Smollett, a stern, angry-looking man in a blue coat and a three-cornered hat.

"Well, Captain Smollett," the squire rumbled, "you sent word that you were displeased. What have you to say?"

"Just this," the captain replied. "I don't like the cruise, and I don't like the men. That's short and sweet."

His tone was so harsh that I crept into a dark corner. *Sit!* I commanded myself silently. *Stay!*

The squire began to splutter, but Dr. Livesey stepped in and said, "Explain yourself, Captain."

The captain said, "I was hired on sealed orders to sail anywhere you told me. I still don't know where

we're headed. But every other man aboard seems to know. I don't call that fair, do you?"

"No," the doctor agreed. "I don't. Where do the men think we're heading?"

"For treasure, sir!" He glared at the other two.

I almost barked out loud in surprise. That was our deepest secret! Who could have blabbed about it? For some reason, I looked right at Squire Trelawney. His face turned very red. "I—I—Livesey, I never told anyone about—"

"Trelawney," the doctor replied, "I know very well how much you like to talk."

"Well," the squire confessed, "I might have let a single little word slip, but—"

"That's enough," the doctor commanded. "Captain, I'll tell you now that we are indeed hunting for treasure."

Captain Smollett nodded grimly. "I don't want to insult you, but neither of you gentlemen knows what you're doing—no more than that boy there."

I put up my ears and cocked my head, thinking, *Captain, don't jump to conclusions about me. I know EXACTLY what I'm doing, thank you very much. I'm sniffing out adventure on the high seas!*

"Where are we mistaken?" Dr. Livesey asked.

The captain shook his head. "You don't know how dangerous it's going to be. A treasure hunt is likely to be a life-or-death matter, and a close run for it. Now, I'll tell you what's what. I've never refused a command, but if you don't take precautions with this crew, I'll ask you to find another captain."

"What's wrong with my crew?" the squire asked.

"I didn't choose them," the captain replied brusquely. "They're too free and easy. They're supposed to be a new crew, but I can tell they've sailed together before. They know one another too well."

"Tell us what precautions you suggest," the doctor said.

The captain looked hard at him. "Well, sir, if you're going through with this voyage, I would suggest this. Take the gunpowder and the guns from the fore hold and store them here instead, under your cabin, where you can control them. Have all your men sleep near your cabin, to help in a pinch."

"Do you think the crew will turn on us?" Squire Trelawney asked with concern, his face having turned as red as a beet.

"If I did, I'd refuse to sail," the captain answered flatly. "So would any officer in his right mind. But if you'll do what I ask, I'll get you to your island safely. If not, please cancel my orders and find yourself another captain."

Humpf! A regular scaredy-cat. Pretty cowardly captain, if you ask me. Which nobody did. Which, as things turned out, was probably just as well. You see, I didn't yet know how close Captain Smollett's warning was to the truth.

"Captain," the doctor said, "you know your business. We will follow your instructions to the letter."

"Thank you, sir," the captain replied.

Well—Captain Smollett seemed to think some exciting times were ahead! I thought I'd play it safe and stick close by Long John Silver's heels. Oops— make that his *heel.*

All the rest of that day we were very busy. I was standing on a barrel, supervising as some men moved the gunpowder, when Captain Smollett saw me and shouted, "Here, ship's boy! Off to the cook and get some work! I'll have no favorites aboard this vessel!"

I went to find Long John, and I assure you, at that moment I hated the captain deeply.

Off to a great adventure! Just what I always wanted! I can't wait to set paws on Treasure Island!

But before I do, maybe I had better get back to Sam, Joe, and David. They're off on an exploit of their own. Hope it's as thrilling as Jim Hawkins's voyage is going to be!

Chapter Four

"**G**uys? Hey, guys? Wait up!" Wishbone ran along behind the three bikes as his pals sped down the path through the woods. It was a stormy, threatening afternoon, and Wishbone kept looking at the sky and worrying. Sam, David, Joe, and Wishbone soon emerged in the clearing before the weathered barn, and Wishbone stared at the old gray building, feeling a funny fluttering in his stomach. "You know, something just told me we'd be coming back here."

Sam parked her bike and stood gazing at the barn, clutching the map to her chest. Thunder rumbled in the distance, but she did not seem to notice. Her smile was determined and stubborn.

Coming up behind her, David muttered, "What are we *doing* here?" He asked the question in a tone that said he would be glad to head for home.

Without looking around, Sam said, "We've got to find that horseshoe."

Joe looked startled. "You heard what my mom and Ms. Gilmore said. The barn's condemned!"

He sounded so upset that Wishbone stared at

him. He could smell Joe's fear of this abandoned old place, its boards creaking in the rising wind of a storm. He tried to give Joe a reassuring glance. "Don't worry, Joe. You have me to protect you!"

You may have heard it said before that dogs can smell fear. Well, it's true. And I'll bet you're wondering what fear smells like to a dog. Unfortunately, I can't tell you—it's a trade secret.

Sam gave Joe a superior look. "We'll be fine," she said. "Don't be scared, guys."

"I'm not scared," David snapped back at once.

Wishbone shook his head. "Come on, David. You say you're not scared, but my nose knows you are. Trade secret, remember?"

Joe's expression became grim and determined. "I'm not afraid, either!" he announced.

Thunder boomed, and Wishbone started to shake. "Well, that's funny. I'm terrified!"

David seemed to catch some of Wishbone's worry. As another clap of thunder came from much closer, he said, "The weather doesn't look so good, guys."

Sam strode toward the barn. "Come on," she said. "I've brought us this far."

Wishbone followed the boys toward the barn as Sam raised the wooden latch and pulled the big door open. Sam's bravery impressed him and made him feel a little better about the adventure. "That's right, Sam. The voyage has begun and you're the captain!" He gulped. "Let's just hope it's a safe trip." He paused at the open barn door and looked anxiously up at the boiling black sky.

The inside of the barn was dark. Wishbone could

smell the faded scent of horses, and lots of decompos-ing hay. His keen ears caught the high-pitched sound of a mouse in a burrow under the wall complaining that they were disturbing its nap. The wood was old, dry, and dusty, but still strong and sound. The "floor" under Wishbone's paws was nothing more than hard-packed dirt. The barn was a very big, creepy, shadowy place, and suddenly he felt very small. He flinched when a branch blown by the wind smashed against the barn's rusted tin roof.

But Sam was looking around as if the barn were a palace. "Can you imagine what this place was like when Blackbeard was alive?" she asked excitedly.

David began to edge toward the door. "Uh, Sam, I think we should go."

Sam turned on him and said, "Look, guys, I'm *not* leaving until I find that horseshoe." The whole barn lit up as a bolt of lightning crashed to earth not far away, and an instant later the air vibrated from a huge explo-sion of thunder. Wishbone was so startled that he yipped, and all the kids gasped.

Joe swallowed hard. "That's it, Sam. We're leav-ing, and you're coming with us."

But at that moment, a strong gust of wind blew the barn door shut with a *boom!* Wishbone heard the latch click into place. "Uh, guys? I hate to bring this up, but I think we're *locked in!*"

David and Joe realized the same awful truth. They hit the door at the same instant and shoved with all their might. No use—the wind had locked them inside the barn, making prisoners of them all.

Thunder crashed again, right overhead. The wind howled.

And a shivering Wishbone realized—"We're trapped!"

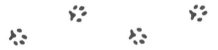

That's the only problem with adventures! They usually give you more than you bargained for—things you don't expect. Oh, you always THINK your plans are going to work out just fine. But then something unexpected happens—just like something unexpected and terrifying happened to Jim Hawkins before he ever got to Treasure Island.

Chapter Five

Our voyage went well. The ship and crew proved to be good, and the captain knew his business. But before we came to Treasure Island, two important events occurred.

First, we lost the mate—big ships have first and second mates, but our schooner had only one, Mr. Arrow. Mr. Arrow was not the best officer in the world. The men wouldn't obey him, and somehow he had found rum to drink. He was unsteady on his feet most days, and no one was much surprised when he vanished at night during a storm. We assumed he had fallen overboard and drowned, leaving us without a mate.

The boatswain—the man in charge of our small boats, rigging, and anchors—was Job Anderson, and he took over some of Mr. Arrow's work. Israel Hands helped, too. He was our coxswain, the one who steered the jolly-boat when the captain wanted to use it. Hands was a careful, wily old sailor who was a good friend of Long John Silver's. I saw Hands often because I spent lots of time in Long John's galley. The galley was the kitchen—my favorite place!

Though he was only the cook, Long John was an important man aboard. The men respected and even obeyed him. He was kind to all, and in particular to me. He never failed to praise my work when I helped him, and often he saved tidbits of especially delicious food for me. Before long, I would have voted for Long John if he ran for admiral.

He had a green parrot as a pet, and he told me all about her. "Now, that bird is maybe two hundred years old, Jim Hawkins. They lives forever, mostly. And she's sailed with pirates, she has. She's been at Madagascar, and to the Malabar coast, and to Portobello—in all the buccaneer ports. She's smelled powder, haven't you, Cap'n?"

And the parrot responded, "Pieces of eight! Pieces of eight!"

Long John laughed. "I call her Cap'n Flint, after the old buccaneer," he told me. "And though she sailed with some of the wickedest scum afloat, she's an innocent bird, so she is. No blood on her claws, matey!"

"Dead men don't bite!" the parrot squawked.

"Hush your pirate talk," Long John scolded. "Forgive her, Jim," he said to me. "She'd carry on that way in front o' the chaplain, so she would."

"Oh, I don't mind her," I said.

Long John laughed and scratched the top of my head. "Good boy, Jim! Good boy!"

Captain Flint's talk really didn't bother me. She was only a bird, after all, and not as smart as a dog, or even as intelligent as the average human. But it was because I was so welcome in the galley that the second important event took place. I learned something dreadful. We had been sailing for weeks when I was hungry one day and went to a huge barrel of apples that always stood open. I didn't particularly like apples, but I had hidden a big soup bone at the bottom. Hey, there's no place to bury a bone on a ship, so I did the best I could!

I had to scamper up onto a keg, hook my paws over the rail, haul myself up, balance on the rail, then hop down inside the barrel to get at my bone. Most of the apples were gone, and as I nosed around on the bottom I heard some men come inside the galley, and one was talking. I recognized Long John's voice, and before he had said a dozen words, I understood that the lives of all the honest men aboard depended upon me alone!

"Flint were captain," Silver was saying, "and I were quartermaster. That was on the *Walrus,* Flint's old ship. Often I've seen her decks running with blood and the ship ready to sink with the weight o' gold!"

In the barrel, I couldn't believe my pointed ears! Long John was saying he'd sailed with Captain Flint. That meant my friend had been a pirate. Still, people can change, I thought.

"Flint was the flower of the flock, they say." It was the voice of Dick, the youngest sailor on the *Hispaniola*—except for me. Dick was about seventeen years old.

"Davis was a cruel pirate, too, I hear," Silver added. "But I never sailed with him—just with England, then with Flint. And I've put aside near three thousand pounds in golden guineas from my voyages, mark ye. Not bad for a man before the mast! And it's all safe in the bank."

"Saving ain't much use to a pirate," the young seaman remarked.

"Not much use for fools, you mean!" Silver returned. "But you're no fool. You're smart as paint. I see that when I first set eyes on you."

Wait a minute, I thought—that's just what he told me! Long John was my best friend on the ship. Or was he?

Silver was talking in his most winning way. "Now, gentlemen of fortune lives rough and they risks swingin', but when a cruise is over, they've hundreds o' guineas in their pockets. Most of 'em throws it away on rum and a good fling, but not Long John. I save it, and I live easy and comfortable. When this voyage is over, I mean to be a rich gentleman. Yet I started just like you, a sailor before the mast!"

Dick sounded worried when he said, "Well, you make it seem easy, Silver. But will the others go along?"

"Most will, ye may lay to that," Silver replied.

I crouched low in the barrel, and even when I smelled my bone I didn't cheer up. "Ye may lay to that" was Long John's sea-going way of saying "It's a sure bet." Did he mean there were more pirates aboard the *Hispaniola*?

Dick must have looked uncertain, because Silver laughed and said, "They'll do what I tell 'em. Some was feared o' Pew, and some was feared o' Flint. But Flint his own self was feared o' me. Ye see how the crew obeys me. Like lambs they are, and they'll do anything I say."

"Well, I tell you," the young man said, "I didn't half a quarter like the idea of mutiny until I talked with you, John. But count me in now, and there's my hand on it!"

"A brave lad ye are, and smart, too!" Silver answered. "And you'll make a fine gentleman o' fortune!"

Something told me that a gentleman of fortune was nothing more than a pirate! I wanted to howl in disappointment!

Just then I heard someone else come into the galley.

Silver said, "Why, hello, Mr. Hands. Dick's with us."

"I know'd he would be," returned the voice of the coxswain, Israel Hands. "Dick's no fool. But Silver, when do we strike?"

Silver flashed out in anger. "When! By the powers, we strike the last moment I can manage, that's when! If I had my way, we'd get the treasure aboard and wait for Captain Smollett to sail us halfway back to England before we did it. But I know this scurvy crew. Ye won't wait, not you. You'll slit their throats for the rum. You're never happy till you're drunk. Split my sides, I've a sick heart to sail with the likes o' ye!"

"Easy, John," Hands mumbled. "We know you're a sort of chaplain, but the rest of the boys likes a fling, so they do."

"Aye," Silver roared, "and where are they now? Pew was like that, and he died a beggar! Flint was, and he died o' rum at Savannah! Oh, a sweet crew, all of 'em, but where are they now?"

Dick asked, "When we do strike, what do we do with them?"

I began to shiver from my nose all the way to my tail. Clearly, we—the doctor, the squire, the captain, and I—were the "them" Silver was talking about. The realization hit me that we were in grave danger!

"Shiver my timbers," Silver said approvingly. "Dick's a lad for business! Well, we could maroon 'em—leave 'em alone on the island with some tools, gunpowder, shot, and food. Cap'n England always did that. Or we could just kill 'em all—that's what Flint would've done, or Billy Bones."

"But what will *we* do?" Dick asked, sounding nervous.

"I'm an easy man," Silver replied, "but this is serious. I vote for death. When I'm in Parlyment, ridin' in my coach, I don't want none o' those in the cabin a-comin' home unlooked for, like the devil at prayers. I say wait, but when the time comes, let her rip! I'll do Trelawney myself—I'll wring his neck with these here hands."

I growled, but very softly. Here I had trusted Long John, but he proved to have no more loyalty to me than a cat! He was trying to turn the whole crew into pirates—and he planned to do dreadful things to the honest men aboard.

Then my ears pricked up in horror as I heard Silver say, "Dick, talkin's left me dry, so it has. Just jump up and get me an apple to wet me pipe."

I looked up and saw Dick's hand reaching into the barrel. Yipe! I curled up as small as I could, tucking my paws under me and curling in my tail. Dick almost had

his fingers on my nose when, from above, the lookout
cried, "Land ho!"

"Thunder!" Silver bellowed. "Let's go look at
Treasure Island, lads!"

To my great relief, I heard a rush of feet and the
clomping of Long John's crutch as they all left. In a
second I jumped up and hooked my paws on the rim

SALTY DOG

of the barrel. I scrambled out and ran to find Dr. Livesey. He was standing by the rail staring at an island, with two low hills, off to the southwest.

"Men!" Captain Smollett called. "Has anyone seen that island before?"

"I have, sir," Silver replied. "A trader I was cook on stopped there for fresh water."

"Do you know the anchorage?"

"Aye, sir," Silver said. "It's on the south, behind a little bit o' rock they calls Skeleton Island. That hill to the north is Foremast Hill, and the big one they calls the Spy-glass. Pirates named everything on the island, because they used to clean their ships and get water there."

"Can you guide us into the anchorage?"

"Aye, sir," Silver replied with a smile. "'Tis a good harbor, to be sure." He saluted and came stumping over to me on his crutch. He patted my head and ruffled my ears, making me shiver when I thought of how he was planning to murder us all. "Ah, Jim," he said, "this island is a sweet spot for a lad. You can swim, climb up them hills, and explore. When ye wants to go ashore, tell old Long John, and he'll make ye a snack to take along!"

I started to say, "Why, that's very nice of you. I'd like a couple of liver sandwiches and—" What was I saying! *No, thank you, Mr. Silver!* I thought grimly.

The cook patted me on the back, then hobbled belowdecks.

I tugged at Dr. Livesey's sleeve and said, "Sir, get the captain and squire to the cabin and send for me. I have dreadful news!"

55

He did not even change expression, but nodded pleasantly. Soon he went inside, and a few minutes later Captain Smollett called all the men on deck. "My lads," he said, "you've done your work well, and the owner, Mr. Trelawney, is pleased with you. He's asked me and the doctor into the cabin to drink to your health and luck, and to have grog served out to you so you can drink to our health and luck. I call that hand-some!"

"So it is!" Long John shouted. "Lads, a good sea cheer for Cap'n Smollett and the gentlemen!"

They all cheered so loudly that you would never have suspected they were plotting murder. As soon as the captain went to the cabin, they sent for me. I hur-ried to them, jumped up into a chair and then onto the tabletop, and in a few minutes I told them the whole frightful story.

When I had finished, Dr. Livesey led them as they solemnly raised their wineglasses in a toast to me. That done, Squire Trelawney said to the captain, "Sir, you were right and I was wrong. What are your orders?"

The captain shook his head. "I never knew a crew that planned a mutiny but gave no sign of it."

"That's Silver," the doctor observed quietly. "He is a remarkable man."

Captain Smollett snorted. "He'd look remark-ably well hanging from a yardarm! But here's the way I see it. We must go ahead because we can't go back. We have some time—at least until the treasure's found. Last, it's clear there must be some honest crewmen still aboard, if Silver's still trying to win men to his side. Now, we can count only on ourselves, Hawkins, and your three servants, Squire. Or can we?"

"Of course we can," Trelawney said at once. "Hunter, Redruth, and Joyce are as close as family!"

"Well, gentlemen," the captain concluded, "we must wait, that's all, and keep a sharp lookout. We can count on seven for our side, and we won't know who else will join us until the fight breaks out. Until then, it's seven of us against nineteen of them."

"Jim can help more than anyone," the doctor said. "He knows all the hands, and he can be our eyes and ears."

"And nose, Doctor," I added proudly.

"Hawkins," the squire said, "I put prodigious faith in you."

It was an enormous responsibility, and odds of seven against nineteen were very unfavorable, indeed. But as a loyal Englishman I had to do my best, for what else could I do?

Chapter Six

The next morning we came to anchor in the bay south of the island. I stood on top of a keg and looked over the rail at it, my nose twitching. Gray woods seemed to cover much of the island, with some yellow streaks of treeless sand. There were hills that rose up like cones, their sides composed of gray rock. The *Hispaniola* rocked quietly at anchor. Not a breath of a breeze stirred. The doctor sniffed at the air, which held an unpleasant smell of rotting leaves and decomposing tree trunks. "I don't know about treasure," he said, "but I'll bet my wig there's fever here."

I nodded my agreement. I never thought land could smell so nasty. Or maybe it was my feeling that something bad was about to happen that made me think the island was an evil place. After all, if the pirates marooned us there, I could spend the rest of my life ashore with not even a dog biscuit to call my own.

As the sun grew hot, the men lay on the deck, grumbling together as they made small talk. They complained when ordered to do any work, and it was clear that their tempers were growing short. Long John worked hard to cheer everyone up, but even he could do little.

In the cabin, the captain said, "Gentlemen, the crew think they can make their way ashore and bang their shins on gold bars sticking out of the ground. Their greed is making them angry. Only one man can calm them down—Silver."

"He's the ringleader!" Squire Trelawney objected.

"But he's as anxious as you or I to smooth things out," Captain Smollett replied. "Let him have the chance. I'll give the men leave to go ashore. If they all go, we'll hold the ship. We can sail away and leave them if we choose, or with the cannon we can fight them off if they try to come aboard again."

"But what if they don't go, Captain?" I asked him.

With an expression of determination, Captain Smollett said, "If none goes, we'll break out our guns and hold the cabin against them all, and God defend the right. Or if some go and some stay, Silver will bring the ones who go ashore back aboard as gentle as lambs, and I think that will keep the others from turning against us."

The squire agreed, and his servants—Mr. Hunter, Mr. Redruth, and Mr. Joyce—came into the cabin and were let in on the secret. They, the squire, and the doctor all armed themselves with pistols, and the captain went on deck to speak to the crew. I followed along and sat on the deck behind him, in his shadow. I was nervous, and my tail twitched as if it had a mind of its own.

"My lads," he said calmly, "you're hot and tired. I'll give you shore leave to enjoy yourselves for a spell.

Take the boats ashore, and I'll fire a gun as a signal for you to return half an hour before sundown."

The crew changed their behavior at once. They gave a cheer that made the tropical birds fly up from the island's jungle with a high squawking, screeching noise that made me want to put my paws over my ears.

With a smile, the captain said, "Mr. Silver, you know the crew as well as anyone. Take charge of organizing the shore-leave groups, if you will." Then he quickly disappeared out of sight.

Silver was obviously their captain now. He divided the crew into units, then began sending the groups into the small boats we called gigs. Silver ordered six of the crew to remain aboard. Soon almost all the others were rowing for shore, and the last few were climbing into a gig they had lowered.

As I stood on deck watching the men prepare that boat, I realized that with six pirates left behind, our group could not take the ship. At the same time, the six pirates could hardly overpower the captain, the doctor, the squire, and the others, armed as they were. I saw no reason why I should stay aboard—not when adventure waited for me on shore! Besides, the doctor had wanted me to be the eyes, ears, and nose for the honest men. And no one had exactly *ordered* me to stay on the ship. And there *was* treasure to dig up. And I *do* love to dig! With all these thoughts twirling around and around in my head, I made my decision and jumped from the deck down into the last boat. No one paid me any mind as I curled up in the bow, and the eager sailors soon rowed us right ashore.

Immediately I jumped out and ran into the

woods, feeling the hot sand beneath my paws. Behind me I heard Silver cry out, "Jim!" But I paid no attention. Usually I'm very obedient, but I'm smart enough not to come when a pirate calls me!

Soon I was far inland, and I looked about with interest. I had never been outside England before. Everything, even the trees, seemed strange and new. All the vegetation smelled different from the kind that I had loved sniffing at home. I even got up close and personal with some.

The day was hot and muggy. I came out onto an open sandy area dotted with pines and willows. There was a land crab crawling there, and I pushed him along with my nose and yipped at him a little. Exploring, I chased strange birds, making them fly up into the trees in red-and-pink blurs of wings. Once I saw a snake that buzzed at me from his place on a rock. I didn't learn until later that it was a deadly rattlesnake. Fortunately, it didn't strike at me—one bite and I'd have been a dead dog!

After an hour or so passed, I heard a dreadful scream from somewhere not far off. My ears pointed straight up, and despite the heat I shivered, for I realized what had happened. The pirates had just killed one of the honest crew members—and I realized that if they caught me, I would suffer the same fate. For the first time I understood exactly how much trouble my adventure had landed me in. What could I do? I had no way of getting back to the *Hispaniola*. I couldn't get into any of the boats if the pirates suspected I had heard that terrible scream and knew what had happened. The *Hispaniola* was anchored too far offshore for me to swim out to it. Anyway, I wasn't much of a swimmer; I could only do a dog-paddle. There seemed nothing left for me but death by starvation or death in the hands of the mutineers.

Just then I heard a rustling behind me. I spun around and saw gravel fall. It rattled and bounded from the side of a steep hill. A moment later something dark and shaggy leaped in front of me. For a second I thought it was a huge monkey, but then I realized it was a man—a skinny man with a great, long, shaggy gray beard; long gray hair that had grown scraggly over his shoulders; and hairy, coarse goatskin clothes that had been patched and tied together. He smelled goaty, too, as if he hadn't had a proper bath for a *long* time. I don't like baths, either, but I think it's good to bathe at least once a year or so!

I was stricken with fear, but he threw himself on his knees in front of me and clasped my paw. "You've come to rescue me!" he croaked in a voice that seemed hoarse as a rusty lock.

"Who are you?" I asked.

"Ben Gunn," he answered. "I'm poor Ben Gunn, I am. I haven't spoke to a soul these three years!"

His voice confirmed that he was English, like myself, though he looked wild. He was tanned dark from the sun, and was as ragged as the poorest beggar in the world. "Three years!" I echoed, almost in disbelief. "Were you shipwrecked?"

"Nay, mate. Marooned. Marooned three years ago, and I lived by eating goats and oysters and wild berries. But my heart is sore for cheese. Many's the night I've dreamed of cheese, toasted mostly."

Uh—sorry, friend, I thought. *I left the Gorgonzola on the* Hispaniola. *Hmm, wild berries. Maybe that was why he acted so weird,* I thought. *Those berries will get you every time.*

Thinking fast, I said, "If you can help me get on board our ship again, I'll give you all the cheese you want."

His face lit up with pleasure. "Ah, you'll be a friend to old Ben Gunn! Yes, I will, says ye. Thank ye kindly, says I. What do ye call yourself, mate?"

"Jim," I told him.

"Jim! Jim!" He seemed pleased. "Well, Jim, I was once a pirate. Aye, and sailed with a devil of a captain—old Flint himself. Well, Jim, back in the year '51, Flint, he buried a treasure on this here island, and then we sailed away. But three year later, Flint died and I gave up being a pirate. I'd had a good, religious mother, ye see, and the life I led hurt my conscience, so it did. But then three year ago, I were on another ship that stopped here for water. I told the men that Flint's treasure were here, and they wanted to find it. Twelve whole days they searched, and when they couldn't find a farthing, they were so angry at me that they left me here with a spade, and a pick-axe, and a musket and powder. And I've been here ever since."

"I'm truly sorry—" I began.

He winked at me. "Sorry for Ben Gunn, says ye. Don't be sorry, says I. Jim, I'm rich!"

He laughed so hard that I felt sure the poor fellow had suffered in his mind from being alone so long.

O-kay, let's admit it. He's crazy as a loon! Good nutrition tip here, gang—lay off the wild berries.

"You don't believe me, says ye," Gunn babbled. "It's true, says I. I'm rich, Jim, rich! But tell me true, Jim, the ship ye come from—is it a pirate ship?"

"No," I said. "There are honest men on her. But I'll tell you true, as you ask me. Some of Flint's old sailors are aboard, and they've mutinied against the rest of us."

"Is there a man with one leg?" he asked, visibly upset.

I felt the fur on my neck bristle at the mention of the same one-legged seaman that Captain Billy Bones had feared so much. Grimly, I responded, "Yes. Long John Silver. He's the ringleader."

Gunn looked sick. "If ye was sent by Long John, I'm as dead as pork, and I knows it."

"No," I said, wagging my tail and trying to look like Ben's best friend. "I'm on the other side." I told him about the squire and the captain.

"You're a good lad, Jim," he said when I had finished. "Trust Ben Gunn to help ye! Tell me, will this squire give me a fair share o' the treasure, if I does? Say, one thousand pounds?"

"I'm sure he would. We were all to share," I explained.

"And would he give me passage home?"

"Yes," I answered. "We'd need you to help sail the ship."

"So ye would!" Gunn cried, delighted. "Jim, you'll go back to your squire and tell him, 'Ben Gunn is a good man. He has a sight more confidence in a gentleman born than in a gentleman o' fortune! And if ye help him, he'll help ye, so he will!' Just have him come out to this clearing, with something white in his hand as a peace token, and him and me will have a talk, we will."

"But I don't have a boat," I said. "How can I get back aboard?"

"That's a hitch, to be sure," he answered. "But I have a boat that I made with my own two hands. I keep her under the white rock—"

A thunderous explosion shattered the stillness. All four of my legs slipped out from under me and made me fall flat on my stomach in surprise. Birds and wild ducks screamed and flew up in a riotous blur all around us.

"What's that?" Gunn cried in alarm.

"The cannon!" I said, getting up off the ground. "They've begun to fight!"

"Come and we'll see!" Gunn said. "Follow the goat path on the left, Jim!"

It was a rough path—maybe all right for goats, but it was hard for a man or a young pup like myself to make his way along it. We ran for a long time and heard more cannon fire. When we broke out onto the top of a hill, suddenly we were looking out across the bay, and there lay the *Hispaniola,* not a quarter of a mile away. Two men were leaning over the cannon, and a third lay on the deck, his shirt red with blood.

"That's Israel Hands aiming!" Gunn cried. "He were Flint's gunner!"

We saw white smoke spout out of the cannon, and a second later the vibration from the explosion hammered into us. Hands seemed to be aiming the weapon directly into the woods.

"Look there!" Gunn said, pointing away from the *Hispaniola*, toward the woods.

I looked and saw a British flag, the Union Jack, flying on a wooden pole. "That must be the captain and the honest men!" I yelped in surprise. What were they doing ashore?

"They're in the old stockade, what the pirates built years ago," Gunn said. "Go to the stockade and join 'em, matey! And don't forget to tell 'em about old Ben Gunn!" He went bounding away and disappeared in a moment.

Having no choice, I ran the other way, crouching to scramble under briars, loping along on all fours in the open spaces. I headed for the stockade and wondered what had caused the captain to flee from his own ship.

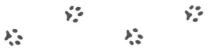

It looks bad for us! What will happen if the buccaneers sail off in the *Hispaniola*? We'll be marooned, just like Ben Gunn. And me without a piece of kibble to my name!

Chapter Seven

If the situation looks bad for Jim Hawkins, just imagine how it must be inside a smelly old barn, with hardly a ray of light coming in. And imagine how scary it is to hear the storm raging outside and realize that you're trapped! That's how we all felt inside the old Trumbull barn. I wish that horse Blackbeard had never worn shoes!

Joe and David crouched side by side, digging the toes of their sneakers into the dirt so they could get a good start. They were all the way at one end of the barn. At the opposite end was the locked door. The two friends looked at each other. They tensed their muscles and then nodded.

Wishbone stared at them, like a coach intent on his star players. "All right, guys. A-one! A-two! CHARGE!"

Both boys sprang forward like sprinters starting a race. They ran at the door as hard as they could. Then, at the same moment, both leaped sideways, slamming their shoulders against the barrier.

Wham!

The door didn't budge, but Joe and David tumbled backward, almost turning a somersault. With a *whump!* they crashed to the straw-covered floor of the barn and lay there flat on their backs, gasping for breath.

Wishbone winced. "Something tells me that hurt."

"No use," David groaned. "We can't break the door down. That was the fifth time we tried. The only thing we're getting is aches and pains."

"I don't think I could take another hit like that," Joe agreed, rubbing his bruised shoulder. He looked at his watch. "We've been trapped here for three hours," he said. "It's going to get dark soon."

Sitting on a pile of straw with her back against the barn wall, Sam mumbled, "It's all my fault." She sounded and looked miserable. She lowered her head and stared at the tips of her sneakers. "I'm really sorry, guys."

Joe pushed himself up. Bits of hay clung to his hair and shirt. "Don't be sorry, Sam. The main thing to do now is just to stay calm."

David got up, too, brushing himself off. "I'd say the main thing to do now is to think of another way of getting out of here," he added.

Wishbone sniffed around the barn floor. He suddenly realized that in one spot he could smell fresh air. With growing excitement, he began to paw the old straw, shoving it aside. A tiny patch of ground was crumbly in that spot. His paws moved faster and faster. Straw and dirt began to fly.

Well, I'd say the main thing to do now is dig! C'mon, everybody! Dig, dig, dig! Go, go, go, go, go!

69

A wisp of straw fell on Sam's shoulder. She brushed it off, then looked down and saw what Wishbone was doing. Her eyes grew wide. "Guys," she yelled, "look at this!"

Wishbone backed away, his tail wagging and his head held high. He looked very proud of himself. "I found a hole!"

Sam said, "He found a hole!"

Wishbone stared at her. "Thank you, even though I said it first. No one ever listens to the dog."

Joe knelt down and looked at it. Wishbone had discovered a small hollow under the wall, its bottom muddy from the rain. The space was far too small for him to wriggle through the way it was, but maybe it could be enlarged. Joe tugged at the wall boards. To his disappointment, they were as solid and unmovable as the barn door.

"Wishbone's trying to help. It's too bad we can't get through that opening," David said.

Joe bit his lip. True, he couldn't squeeze under the wall, nor could David or Sam. None of them could, except— "Wishbone can fit!" Joe yelled. "He can run for help!"

David nodded, his expression excited but thoughtful. "I guess so, but how will they know we're trapped here? How can we send a message?"

Sam's face lit up. "He can take the map!"

Joe grinned. "Great idea, Sam. Does anybody have a pen, a pencil—anything to write with?"

"Not me," David said, slapping his pockets. "Sam?"

"No, but it doesn't matter!" Sam exclaimed. "Ms. Gilmore gave me this map. It's got her handwriting on it. She'll recognize it if Wishbone can get it to her, and she'll know it came from us!" She held out the folded map. "Here, Wishbone. Take this and go."

Feeling truly heroic, Wishbone clamped his teeth on the map and gave his friends a reassuring look. "Don't worry, guys, I won't let you down!" He thought of all the dog heroes he had heard about or seen on television. "Eat your heart out, Lassie!" Turning, he squirmed down into the hole. It was a tight fit, but he pushed himself through.

Raindrops pelted him as soon as he had wriggled out of the barn. Lightning flashed overhead. Thunder growled. Wishbone ignored it all, knowing his friends were counting on him. Taking a deep breath, he began to run for home at top speed. It was Wonder Wishbone to the rescue!

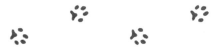

Close calls and narrow escapes—that's what adventure is all about! Just like the ones Jim Hawkins had when he left Ben Gunn and headed to the old stockade on Treasure Island.

Chapter Eight

Even with four good legs, it took me a long time to pick my way through the woods to the stockade. Once, near sundown, I came to another clearing and glimpsed the *Hispaniola* again. The Jolly Roger, the skull-and-crossbones flag of piracy, was flying from her mast. Ugh! There was nothing appetizing about the look of *those* bones! Even as I gazed out toward the sea, there came another red flash and puff of smoke, and another cannon ball whistled through the air.

I heard the pirates who had gone ashore singing and shouting loudly in the marshes off to the right. I judged that was where they had camped for the night. Circling away from there, I got lost and came out near the shore behind the stockade. From there I saw a huge white rock, probably the one that Ben Gunn had mentioned. It was where he kept his boat, I remembered. Finally I skirted the woods until I picked up the right track. Sure enough, I found the familiar scents of the doctor, the squire, and the captain; following them, I soon came to the stockade.

It was on a small, sandy hill, with a clearing

around it. A palisade—a fence constructed of tree trunks sharpened at the top ends—enclosed a blockhouse at the top of the hill. The house was about twenty feet square and made of thick logs, and it had only one door. Narrow windows pierced the walls. The blockhouse also had loopholes, which were openings that would allow the defenders inside the blockhouse to fire muskets at anyone attacking. The fence was sturdy, and a grown man could never hope to squeeze between the trunks, but I had no trouble at all. The doctor was standing in the doorway and saw me approaching. He sang out a welcome, and in a moment I was inside.

The doctor told me their story. They had settled down to wait, but the six hands left aboard looked surly and cross. Redruth, the squire's butler, told them he had seen me jump into one of the gigs. Worried about me, the doctor decided that he and Hunter would go ashore in the captain's jolly-boat to see if they could find me. They came upon the stockade instead, and the doctor saw that it was a good, strong fort that could be defended. As he and Hunter were returning to the ship, they heard the dying scream of a man and realized that the pirates on shore had killed someone.

The people on board the *Hispaniola* had heard it, too. The six pirates turned on the captain and his party, but they in turn drove the mutineers under the forward hatch. When the doctor scrambled aboard, the captain decided their best chance was to take gunpowder and weapons and as much food as they could carry to the stockade. They could hold out there against the pirates. They made several trips in the jolly-boat, and just before the last one, the sailor Abraham Gray broke away from the mutineers in the hold. "I'm with you, sir," he had said, joining the captain.

The cannon blasts and gunfire that Ben Gunn and I had heard came from Israel Hands and the others trying to sink the jolly-boat on her last trip in. Squire Trelawney, a good shot, had tried to drop Hands, but he had hit one of the others instead. In the end, Hands had failed to hit the jolly-boat with cannon fire, but the boat took in water trying to land, spoiling some food and gunpowder.

The captain, squire, doctor, and others hurried to the stockade. A party of pirates tried to cut them off, but they came too late. In the fighting that followed, poor old Redruth was killed. The pirates were beaten back, though, and the loyal crew had taken the stockade as their own. Captain Smollett raised the Union Jack and prepared to defend his new command post just as if it were a ship. And a good enough place it was, the doctor finished, on healthy ground. It was high and dry, with its own spring bubbling up to supply fresh water.

In turn, I told them all about Ben Gunn and his peculiar message.

"The man must be mad!" the squire exclaimed.

"We shall see," Dr. Livesey said. "I have a nice piece of Parmesan cheese, very nourishing, that I brought from the ship. If Ben Gunn can help us, that cheese shall be his!"

That's fine for old Ben, Doctor. Now, did you

75

happen to bring any ginger snaps ashore? No? Oh, well, like Ben, I suppose I can dream about my favorite snack!

As night fell, Captain Smollett organized us into watches and gave us jobs to do. Some were assigned to cut firewood, and others to stand guard, while he and Abraham Gray dug a grave to bury Mr. Redruth. We kept so busy that we hardly had time to worry or be afraid.

After supper, the squire, the doctor, and the captain conferred for a long time. Our main problem was that the last load carried by the jolly-boat, the one we lost when it sank, contained most of our food. We couldn't hold out for long. However, as the captain pointed out, the odds had improved. Abraham Gray had come over to our side, and in the fighting, three of the pirates had been killed and at least two wounded. "From nineteen they're down to fifteen at most," the captain declared. "Our best hope is to hold the fort and pick off the survivors one by one until they give up or sail off to plunder ships."

"We have two allies helping us," the doctor observed. "Rum and the climate. Between drinking and fever, I'll stake my wig that the mutineers will lose yet more men without a shot being fired."

I was dead tired that night and slept like a log. The others let me sleep late the next day. Just as I woke up, I heard Hunter shout, "One of them's coming with a flag of truce!"

I sprang up at once, jumped onto a brandy cask, and looked out one of the loopholes of the fort. Sure enough, waving a white flag, Silver himself stood not far from the stockade. I felt very strange. He had been my good friend, and yet now I was so afraid of him that my tail tucked itself between my hind legs. As he stood there, he smiled and waved his flag, looking just like the good old Long John who had won my loyalty.

"Keep indoors, men," Captain Smollett commanded. "Ten to one this is a trick." He stepped out of the blockhouse and cried, "Who goes there? Stand still, or we'll fire!"

"Flag o' truce!" Silver shouted back.

The captain turned and said, "Dr. Livesey, watch the north side. Jim, the east. Gray, west. Everyone else, load muskets." He turned again and called out, "And what do you want with your flag of truce?"

"Captain Silver, sir, come to make terms!" he shouted.

"Don't know any Captain Silver!" the captain snapped.

But Long John did not seem offended, and he gave his broadest smile. "'Tis me, sir. These lads have elected me captain, after ye deserted the ship. All I ask is safe passage in and out, and one minute after I leave before ye fire a gun."

"I don't want to speak to you," the captain said. "But if you want to talk, come ahead. We won't start the fighting."

"A word from you's enough!" Long John shouted, sounding cheerful. He hobbled to the stockade, threw his crutch over the wall, then hoisted himself over the fence, dropping safely over. He had a terrible time trudging up the sandy hill, for his crutch kept sinking into the soft surface. Despite my fear, I began to feel sorry for him. What must it be like to have only one leg instead of four sturdy limbs? But at last he arrived and saluted, panting hard.

"You'd better sit down," Captain Smollett said.

"Well, Cap'n," the sea-cook responded, "I'll be glad to sit and jaw, but someone will have to give me a hand up again, because of my timber leg. My service to ye all, gentlemen, and good mornin' to ye, Jim!"

"If you have anything to say, say it," Captain Smollett ordered in a commanding voice. I realized he'd have been a great obedience-school teacher!

"Right you are, Cap'n," Silver replied, sitting down. "Duty is duty. Look here, one of ye did some bloody work last night. I won't say it wasn't our fault. We didn't keep as sharp a watch as we should have. But is it right, now, for somebody to sneak into our camp in the dark and strike a poor sleepin' sailor with a hand-spike? He were dead by the time I waked up, he were."

What? I looked up at Captain Smollett's face in surprise, and my sharp ears caught a little murmur of astonishment from the people inside the blockhouse. I didn't think Silver heard it, though, and the captain did not act as if he were at all surprised. He simply said, "That's not what you came to talk about, Silver."

"No," Silver agreed. "But here it be. We want that treasure, and to get it we want that map."

"You won't get either one," the captain replied flatly. "We've been on to you for a long time, Silver."

Silver's face darkened like a thundercloud. "If Abe Gray talked about our plans—"

"Avast there!" Captain Smollett boomed. "Gray told me nothing, and I asked him nothing."

"I takes your word on that, Cap'n," Silver said.

For a while they sat side by side, like old companions, glancing at each other from time to time. It was as good as watching a play to gaze at them. I had figured out by then that the mysterious attacker who had killed one of the pirates in the night must be none other than Ben Gunn. That was his way of proving his friendship to us. *Brr*— I was glad Ben was on our side and not theirs!

"Well," Silver said after a while, "give us the map, and I'll give ye my word of honor to divide our food with ye, man for man. Then when we leave, I'll speak to the first ship we meet, and tell 'em to come and rescue ye. That's fair all around. Handsomer ye couldn't look to get, not ye."

Captain Smollett rose to his feet. "Is that all?"

"Every last word, by thunder!" Long John answered emphatically. "Refuse that, and you've seen the last of me but musket balls!"

"Then here's my answer," the captain replied sternly. "If you'll give up, one by one, I'll clap you in irons and take you home to a fair trial in England. If you won't, my name's Alexander Smollett, I've flown the king's colors, and I'll see you all to Davy Jones. You can't find the treasure, and there's not a man among you who knows how to set a course and navigate the

80

ship. You're in a bad way, Silver. Now tramp off and tell your men what I've said."

Silver's expression was a picture of fury. His eyes bulged with anger. "Give me a hand up!"

"Not I," the captain replied.

"Who'll give me a hand up?" Silver roared.

After hearing his treachery with my own pointed little ears, I wouldn't lift a paw to help Silver. Not one of us moved.

Silver had to crawl on all fours—or on all three—until he reached the fence and could pull himself upright. He turned and spat. "Before an hour's up, I'll storm this blockhouse," he threatened. "Them that die will be the lucky ones!" In a moment he had hauled himself back over the fence. Soon afterward he had disappeared into the woods.

The captain turned, his face serious. "Stand by for action," he announced. "And get back to your posts!"

He scolded us for deserting our places, all but Gray, who had stood faithfully by his loophole.

When he had finished issuing orders, the captain said, "Now Silver will attack. I purposely made him angry so he would. But we can beat them, if you will only obey orders and keep your heads."

An hour passed slowly by. We had breakfast by ones and twos, and then we returned to watch the woods. Suddenly Joyce cried out, "I see a man, sir! They're coming!" Several shots rang out from the woods just then, and Joyce whipped his musket up and fired.

"Did you hit your man?" the captain asked.

"No, sir," Joyce replied, reaching for a fresh musket.

"Next best thing is to tell the truth. Load his musket again, Hawkins."

The captain had everyone report on the number of shots he had seen. It was clear that most of the pirates were to the north, and the main attack would come from that direction.

The captain put Gray and the squire on that side. "Now we have to keep them outside the fence," he said. "If they get close to the blockhouse, they'll fire through the loopholes and we'll be trapped."

Just at that moment we heard the pirates shout. Firing broke out again. A party of pirates stormed the fence and scrambled over it like monkeys. Squire and Gray fired again and again, and three of the opposition fell. But four charged the blockhouse, and one shot came whistling through a loophole and struck Mr. Joyce dead on the spot.

"All hands out in the open!" Captain Smollett ordered.

We seized cutlasses—short, curved swords—from a waiting stack and went rushing out, all but Hunter. One of the pirates had grabbed the barrel of Hunter's musket and had slammed it into his chest with a smashing blow, knocking him unconscious to the floor.

The rest of us were outside in a moment. I felt the squire brush by my tail behind me, and right in front was the doctor. He fought off a pirate and chased him down the hill. I was conscious of the sun hot on my fur and the sickening scents of gunpowder, steel, and blood boiling over everything.

"Round the house, lads!" the captain shouted.

I heard more gunfire from the woods, three or four shots. None seemed to hit anything. The tall sailor Job Anderson suddenly was in front of me, his sword flashing in the sunlight as he ran up the sandy hill. He struck at me and might have cut me in half if I had not fallen and rolled paws over head in the soft sand and down the slope. As it was, Anderson staggered, off balance, and Abraham Gray cut him down before he could recover.

I got onto all four feet and realized that in the few seconds it had taken me to roll downhill everything had changed and we had won the confrontation. The pirate Anderson lay dead, and the doctor's attacker was stretched out, too. Another pirate had been shot down as he tried to fire into the house. The last one of the four who had rushed the blockhouse had clambered back over the fence and was beating a hasty retreat. My keen ears heard distant shouts and curses from the woods as the pirates ran away.

Still, in the open we were good musket targets, so we rushed back up the hill and inside the blockhouse. "Fire at anyone you see!" ordered the captain.

But we could see no one.

"It's over," the squire said. Then he turned to the doctor. "Livesey, the captain's wounded."

I looked and saw that the captain's uniform was wet with blood on the shoulder and the right leg. He had the coppery smell of blood all over him, along with the sweaty scent of exhaustion.

"Have they run?" Captain Smollett gasped.

83

"All that could," the doctor said, helping the captain lie down. "But five will never run again!"

"Five!" the captain exclaimed. "That leaves only nine of them. Not so bad, my lads."

But we had lost men, too. Poor Hunter, who had been Squire Trelawney's gardener, never recovered, and he died without saying another word. The squire's valet, Mr. Joyce, had fallen, shot through the head, dead instantly.

In the dark interior of the blockhouse, the doctor tended busily to the wounded captain. Gray and Squire Trelawney kept watch at the loopholes, slumping wearily against the log walls. If, as the captain said, we were five to nine, we were a little better off than before. Still, the captain was so badly wounded that it was really only four to nine. The odds did not make me feel any better.

Chapter Nine

Jim Hawkins was really brave! Just as brave as Joe, Sam, David, and I had to be when we were trapped in the Trumbull barn. As soon as I had squeezed through the hole, I made a bee-line—or is that a dog-line? Anyway, I ran straight for home, with lightning flashing and thunder booming! I was one tired pup when I came charging down our street and saw a car turn into the drive. Mr. Walter Kepler, Sam's dad, jumped out and ran to the door. Although I was still half a block away, my sensitive ears could hear what was going on at the house.

Ellen Talbot put down the phone and said, "David's dad is out searching everywhere. Wanda, where could they be?"

In a worried voice, Wanda Gilmore said, "Oh, Ellen, I don't know. What are we going to do?"

Just then someone knocked on the door, and Ellen rushed to open it. It was Mr. Kepler. "Any word?" he asked.

"No, Walter," Ellen said miserably. Thunder rum-

bled overhead from a dark, ragged sky. "That's it. I'm calling the police."

Wishbone, running as fast as his weary limbs could move, saw the door closing in front of him. He put on an extra burst of speed. "Who needs the police? You've got— Hey!" Too late. The door had closed firmly in his face. Gripping the map tightly in his teeth, Wishbone stood on his hind legs and stretched up his front paws. He was about two feet too short to reach the doorbell.

Why don't they put doorbells a little lower? Well, maybe I can't ring, but I know one way to get their attention! The old reliable scratch at the door. Scratch! Scratch! Scratch! "Helllooo! Wishbone-gram! Important message here!"

He clawed frantically at the wooden door for a few seconds, and then Ellen opened it. "Wishbone!" she exclaimed as he ran in.

Wishbone did a hurry-up-why-don't-you dance, jumping and circling and waving the map for all he was worth. Wanda Gilmore stooped over him. "What's that he's got in his teeth?"

Wishbone held it up toward her. "Issa map! Issa map! Go on an' take it. Issa clue!"

At last Wanda reached for the folded paper and took it from Wishbone's sharp-toothed grasp. "Why, it's a map of Oakdale!" she exclaimed.

Wishbone barked anxiously. "Come on—don't you understand what this means?"

"What's he doing with a map?" Mr. Kepler asked.

"Wishbone, where are Joe and his friends?" Ellen inquired at the same moment.

Wishbone stared at her. "Nobody *ever* listens to the dog. They're in trouble! Look at the map!"

Wanda had finally unfolded the map. "Why, this is *my* map! I wrote the directions for finding the—" She looked up. "Ellen, get your car keys. I know where they are!"

Breathing a sigh of deep relief, Wishbone hurried after Ellen, his nails clicking on the floor. "I'm glad we're driving back. That's a long run, even with four legs! I don't suppose we have time for a doggie ginger snap—"

A burst of lightning and a terrible crash of thunder made Wishbone flinch.

"Never mind! I can't think of eating when Joe is trapped in that spooky place! But when we get back, it's ginger snap time!"

Ellen had pulled on her raincoat, and Wishbone

trotted beside her as she, Wanda, and Mr. Kepler all piled into the family car.

"Hang on, gang! We're coming to the rescue!"

I didn't know it at the time, but things had gone from bad to worse at the barn. It was out of the frying pan and into the fire for my friends—literally! But at the moment, I was full of excitement as we drove through the storm. I felt just like Jim Hawkins, who, like me, found more adventure than he bargained for.

Chapter Ten

On Treasure Island, the pirates had had enough of fighting. The doctor even treated one of the wounded pirates right along with Captain Smollett. That night, I tried to sleep. I turned around three times and finally curled up in a corner. But an idea came into my head and wouldn't let me drift off.

I would slip out to the schooner and see if I could cut her adrift! *Without the* Hispaniola, *the pirates would be helpless and would have to give up,* I thought. The more I considered the idea, the better it seemed to me. I'd find adventure *and* be a hero!

Only Abraham Gray was awake. He was outside, slowly pacing around and around the blockhouse, keeping watch. Of course, I could have awakened Captain Smollett and asked his permission to go, but he was wounded and needed his sleep. Besides, he might have commanded me to stay in the blockhouse. I was so excited by the opportunity for adventure that, strange as it seemed, it never occurred to me that my friends might think I was running away out of fear. All I could think about was returning to them as a hero!

So, getting up in the dark, I stuck a loaded pistol into my belt and took a pouch of powder and shot. When Gray was on the other side of the blockhouse, I slipped away to the white rock. Soon I found Ben Gunn's little boat and rowed myself out to the *Hispaniola*. Imagine my surprise when I discovered that the two pirates left on board had fought each other in a drunken rage! One was dead. The other, Israel Hands, was badly wounded. So I took command of the ship! Captain Jim Hawkins, that's me!

"Are you comfortable, Mr. Hands?" I asked the gunner, who lay against a bulkhead with his shoulder all bloody.

"If that doctor was aboard," he said, "I'd be right enough, but I don't have no good luck. Where'd you come from, boy?"

"I've come to take the ship. You can call me 'captain,'" I told him. "And I won't fly these pirate colors, so down comes the Jolly Roger!" I grabbed the line in my teeth and hauled down their black flag of piracy. Seizing it in my mouth, I growled, gave it three good shakes, and threw it overboard. I said, "God save the king, and that's the end of Captain Silver!"

Hands frowned at me. "Well, I reckon you want to get ashore. Let's strike a bargain. Give me some food and drink and an old scarf to tie up my wound, and I'll tell you how to sail the schooner. That's fair, ain't it?"

"Fair enough," I told him, "as long as we sail her to the far side of the island and out of the pirates' reach." The *Hispaniola* was held by only one of her three anchors. I could not pull it up, but I was able to chew through the rope in just a few minutes. Then I hauled up the jib—the small sail in the front—and the foresail. After doing that, I stood at the tiller, the lever that steered the ship. I could push it left with my paws, and the rudder that it was attached to would make the ship turn right. When I had the *Hispaniola* heading north, I tied the tiller down and went below to get Hands a morsel of food, something to drink, and a bandage for his shoulder. Of course, while I was in the galley I got a bite or two for myself. Nothing fancy. Just a ship's biscuit and a small piece of dried beef, which was hard as a good bone, to tide me over.

Hands perked up as soon as he had eaten, and I felt better after my own snack. With only two small sails and not much wind, sailing went slowly. We slipped northward along the coast as the sun came up. By noon we had turned east around the point of the island. Then we had to tack south—**that means we had to sail in a zigzag path, the way I run when I chase a confused cat.**

All this time Hands told me what lines to pull on, which way to push the tiller, and in general made himself useful. In the afternoon, we ran into a cove called North Inlet, where the water was calm. With a good breeze, we steered for a sandy beach.

"You can't handle the port-side anchor," Hands told me. "Nor can I, with this here wound. So your best bet is to run her in fast and beach her at high water. You can tie her down with a couple of lines lashed to trees, and she'll be safe and sound until you want to get her to sea again."

This was exciting! I gripped the tiller hard in my

teeth and felt my tail wagging with the thrill of command.

Hands gave me instructions. "Steady," he cautioned. "Starboard a little. Now, luff, my hearty, luff!"

I knew that he meant to move the tiller so that the sails lost their wind, so I pulled it to the left with all my might. The *Hispaniola* turned right, or starboard, and glided ahead at top speed. I heard her bows crunch in the sand. Then everything gave a jerk, the deck tilted, and we stopped moving. I had beached the schooner! A sudden movement caught my eye, and when I turned with a big grin on my face, I saw Hands lunging toward me with a huge knife.

I yelped and pushed hard with my hind legs, leaping up into the rigging. Hanging on by my teeth and toenails, I climbed to the yardarm, the wooden pole that supports the sail, where I sat with my back against the mast.

Hands, rage on his face, came climbing up after me, his knife clenched between his teeth. With his wounded shoulder, he climbed slowly, grunting at each step. I drew my pistol, cocked it, and pulled the trigger. Nothing happened! I realized the powder must have become damp. I frantically began to change the powder as Hands pulled his way up, hand over hand.

He was only ten feet below me when I pointed the pistol and said, "Who's top dog, now, Mr. Hands? Stop right there, or I'll fire!"

Hands hooked his bad arm through the rigging and took the knife out of his mouth with his other hand. "I reckon you've won," he said bitterly. "But it's

hard for a master sailor like me to have to give up to a youngster like you, Jim."

I started to reply, when back went his hand over his shoulder, and he whipped the dagger forward, throwing it right at me. I felt it snag my hide, and my paw jerked on the trigger. The pistol went off. Hands screamed and fell.

To this day I don't know if I hit him or if he lost his balance when he threw the knife. He tumbled forty feet down, hit the rail with a crack that must have broken his neck, and fell into the water, where he sank. That was the last I saw of Mr. Hands.

The knife burned into my hide, and it pinned me to the mast through my clothing. I reached for it with my mouth to pull it out, shivering, and my shaking broke me free of it. The blade had barely nicked my coat and had been holding me by just a pinch of skin and fur. I climbed down and took a minute to lick and bandage my wound. Then, with much difficulty, I lowered the sails and tied lines to the trees, as Hands had suggested.

By then the sun was going down. I knew the stockade was a long way to the south, so I made myself a few beef sandwiches to keep me going and set off at a trot through the trees.

Night came on, but a bright full moon rose above Spy-glass Hill. Still, it was nearly midnight by the time I came to the clearing where the stockade stood, with no sentry in sight. Something smelled fishy. Or should I say piratey? I should have paid more attention to my nose. My nose ALWAYS knows!

Creeping softly up to the fence, I squeezed through a tiny gap. No one challenged me, and I couldn't help thinking that our men should have kept a better lookout. When I thought how they would smile when they heard how I had stolen the ship right out from under the pirates' noses, I felt as proud of myself as a purebred who'd just won a blue ribbon.

Padding quietly, I went inside the blockhouse. It was too dark to see, but I stepped on something soft—a sleeper's leg.

Then, all of a sudden, a shrill voice broke out of the darkness: "Pieces of eight! Pieces of eight! Pieces of eight!"

Silver's green parrot, Captain Flint! All around me sleeping men were jolted awake, and I heard Long John Silver's voice cry out: "Who goes there?"

I started to run, but someone grabbed me. "Bring a torch!" he yelled, and in a few seconds someone struck a light.

Long John held me by the scruff of the neck. The other pirates stared at me. I felt my tail curl between my legs.

I had walked right into the pirates' lair, and now they had me as their prisoner. I was out of the frying pan, all right, and into a very hot fire!

Chapter Eleven

While Silver held me, five of the other pirates stared. Those five were the only ones left alive. One of them wore a bloodstained bandage around his head and lay on the floor, as if he were too weak to stand. The parrot perched on Long John's shoulder, sneering at me. Okay, okay, I know birds can't sneer. But if they could, she would have been doing it with glee.

Long John let go of me and stepped back. "So, Jim Hawkins, ye dropped in for a friendly visit. Shiver my timbers, lad, you've got spirit!"

I turned away and put my nose in the air, pointedly ignoring him.

Silver only laughed. "Jim, I've always liked ye. Ye reminds me of myself when I was young and handsome. Now, I'll tell ye what. Ye just join with us and take your share o' the treasure, and become a gentleman. You'll have to, come to that. Cap'n Smollett's a fine seaman, but he's stiff on duty, and he thinks you've deserted, ye see, so you'll have to steer clear o' the cap'n. And the doctor himself is clean against ye.

He called ye an ungrateful scamp for runnin' away. So ye can't go back, because your own people won't have ye. Unless ye want to start another ship's crew on your own—which would be lonely—you'll have to join with Cap'n Silver. So what does ye say, lad?"

My ears had pricked up, because Silver had told me something startling. My friends were still alive! At the moment, that was more important to me than the terrible news that they thought I had deserted them. The other pirates began to grumble and mutter among themselves, but I looked back at Silver. "You want my answer?"

Silver nodded gravely. "I won't hide the fact that you're in danger, Jim, for these lads have no reason to like ye. But it's your choice. If my offer be pleasin' to ye, join us. If not, Jim, you're free to answer no—free and welcome. So what does ye say, my fine young man?"

My heart was beating fast, and I was beginning to pant. "First tell me why you're here in the stockade and where my friends are."

One of the pirates snarled a curse, but Silver held up his hand for silence. "Ye will batten down your hatches until you're spoke to, friend," he said sternly. Then to me, he said, "Yesterday mornin' the doctor came to us with a flag o' truce. The first thing he told us was that the schooner had sailed off before dawn, and when we looked, so it had. Dr. Livesey said as cool as ye please, 'I think you'd better bargain with us, Silver.' We bargained, and we agreed to let 'em go if they'd give up the stockade. So that's that. They've left, and I don't know where they've gone."

"All right," I said. I stood up tall on my four legs and held my head back in defiance of them all. "Then before I give you my answer about joining, let me tell you a thing or two. First, you're in bad shape—you've lost the ship, lost the treasure, and lost most of your men. Second, I did it all! I was in the apple barrel the night we sighted land and I heard your whole evil plot. Last night I rowed out and cut the *Hispaniola*'s cable and sailed her to where you'll never see her again. I'll never join you. Now kill me if you please, but if you let me live, I'll do my best to keep you from hanging when you come to trial for piracy. Mr. Silver, you're the best man here. If these men kill me, please try to tell the doctor so he can let my mother know what happened to me."

With a strange half-smile, Silver nodded and said, "I'll do my best for ye, Jim."

One of the sailors drew his knife and cried, "What are we waiting for? Cut his throat!"

Silver's eyes blazed. "Avast there! Who are ye to decide that, Tom Morgan? I'm cap'n here! Cross me and you'll regret it. Ye may lay to that! Put away your knife, Morgan, and sit!"

One thing I'll say for Long John Silver: he knew how to give commands. I obediently sat myself when he snapped that order.

Morgan did as he was told, but the others grumbled. "Tom's right," one said.

Another one added, "I'll be hanged if you'll tell me what to do, John Silver."

"Mutiny, is it?" Silver roared. "Ye knows how it is with gentlemen o' fortune. Let one o' you step outside with me, give us a cutlass each, and I'll see the color of his insides! Who shall it be?" When no one answered, Silver shook his head. "I thought not. I'm cap'n here because I'm the best man by a long sea mile. I like that boy. I've never seen a better or a braver one—he's more a man than any two o' you rats. Any lubber who lays a hand on Jim Hawkins will answer to me."

Morgan swallowed hard. "We got our rights. This crew's dissatisfied, so we'll step outside for a council, accordin' to rules." And one by one they went.

Silver sat on a brandy keg and leaned close to whisper to me. "Look here, Jim, you're within half a plank o' death or—even worse—torture. They're goin' to throw me out as cap'n. But I'll stand by ye, and ye stand by me."

I tilted my head and cocked my ears at him. "You mean, save you from hanging?"

"Aye, so I do. I'll save your life from 'em, and when the time comes, you save Long John from swingin'."

"I'll do what I can," I told him, and gave him my paw on it.

"Good enough, by thunder!" Silver shook my paw. "You're a plucky lad, Jim. I know you've got the schooner somewhere safe and that if we finds the squire, you'll speak up for me. Ah, Jim, I wish I'd met ye when we was both five years younger. With me to teach ye how to be a proper gentleman o' fortune, we could have done a power o' good together."

He had no time to say more, because the crew came marching back into the stockade just then, in an ugly mood. One of the five men came up to Silver, holding a piece of paper in his hand. It shook with his fear. It smelled of charcoal and had a rough, round black spot drawn on it. I had seen a paper just like that in the hands of poor old Billy Bones!

"Step up, Dick," Silver said. "I know the rules. I won't hurt ye."

The man handed Silver the paper, then hastily backed away to join his friends.

Silver looked at it. "The black spot. I thought so. Where'd ye get the paper?" He turned it over. "What's this? You've gone and cut this out of a Bible. What fool cut a Bible?"

"It was Dick," Morgan replied.

Silver shook his head. "Then Dick will have no more luck in this life, and ye may lay to that. But let's go by the rules. What's your complaint? You, George Merry—tell me what it is ye object to."

George, a tall blond pirate with yellowish-brown eyes, said, "First, you've made a mess of this cruise. Second, you let the enemy out of this trap. Third, you wouldn't let us kill 'em when they was leavin' this stockade under their flag o' truce. And fourth, there's this here boy."

"Is that all?" Silver asked quietly.

"It's enough!" Merry shouted. "We'll all swing because of your bunglin'!"

Silver rose from where he sat and towered above them all, his face glistening in the torchlight. "Then I'll answer them four points. *I* made a mess o' this cruise? Every man here knows what I wanted! If ye'd done that, we'd have been safe aboard the *Hispaniola* right now, every man alive, with the treasure in the hold! But who had to go ashore and hunt for treasure that first day, leaving the ship? It was Anderson and Morgan and you, George Merry!"

The four others backed away some distance from Merry, who scowled in fury. He looked like a mangy cur trying to work up the nerve to get in a dog fight.

Silver was sweating. He came a step closer to them, and they fell back. "And as long as I'm cap'n, my crew will respect a flag o' truce! For your fourth point, young Jim— Shiver my timbers, if you knew how close ye all are to swingin', you'd treat that boy like royalty! He's the only one who could testify on your side, ye lubbers! Finally, just to show that I ain't bungled everything, there's this!" He reached inside his coat, pulled out a folded piece of parchment, and threw it to the ground. "Ye lost the ship, but I found the treasure! There's the treasure map—that I got from the doctor! Now I'm done with ye! Elect a cap'n ye like!" He turned, put his hand on my back, and led me across the blockhouse.

The pirates had grabbed the map. One of them said, "That's it! I recognize Flint's handwriting!"

Another one cried out, "Silver's our cap'n! I say he stays!"

Two more cheered.

Silver ruffled the fur on my head and winked at me. I could see how relieved he was. "Then you'll have to wait a little longer to be cap'n, George Merry," he said. "Now, I'm not a vengeful man, so we'll let bygones be bygones. Jim, you'll bunk in the corner there, and I'll sleep right here so that any swab who wants to get at ye will have to step over me—and I sleep light."

With that, we all turned in, though you can guess I hardly slept at all. Every time I put my head down on to my paws, a pirate would moan or snore, and I'd jerk my head back up, my nerves tingling. It was a long night I spent lying there, listening to the pirates' uneven breathing and smelling their familiar scent of fear and anger.

Where did Silver get that map? And why would Dr. Livesey give it up? There's a mystery here! And there's danger—danger just as great as Joe and his friends faced when something new happened in the old barn.

Chapter Twelve

A s Ellen drove us toward the barn, events were occurring. I didn't know about them at the time, but later I found out just how hot the old barn had become for my friends.

Joe, David, and Sam had been sitting for hours. The barn was clammy and smelled moldy. The storm just wouldn't stop. It had rained a little, but then the rain slackened. Next the wind had risen, and all the time the lightning and thunder kept up, sounding like a battle raging just outside the sturdy old weathered walls.

David stood and said, "I'm going to take another look around. There's got to be another way out."

Joe sighed. "I think we would have found it in the first five times we looked," he said. "We've searched everywhere. The only ways out are the door and the hole. If we had a shovel, we might be able to dig our way out—after about two or three hours."

"Wait a minute," Sam murmured thoughtfully. "We haven't looked everywhere."

"Sam, we've been over every inch of this place," Joe replied, sounding exasperated.

"No, we haven't," she told him. "There's the loft."

They all looked up. "There's no way up," David pointed out.

"There has to be," Sam insisted. She stood up and stamped her feet. Her legs had gone to sleep, and now they tingled as the feeling came back. "Barn lofts have doors in them, don't they?"

"Sure, I guess so," Joe admitted. "But David's right. I don't see any way of getting up there."

"I think I saw a ladder in the back," Sam answered hopefully. "Come on."

It was very dark in the barn, with just a little light leaking in through the cracks between the old boards. The three friends groped through the dimness until they came to the back wall. There, lying on the ground, was the worst-looking ladder Sam had ever seen. It was home-made, with many short planks nailed to two very long ones.

"Here it is!" Sam said triumphantly.

Joe leaned over to help her lift it. He grabbed a rung—and it pulled loose from its rusty nails at the first tug. "Sam, this isn't a ladder," he said. "It's a broken leg waiting to happen. The wood's rotten."

"We've got to try it," Sam insisted, tugging. "Help me."

David grabbed the other end. "I think Joe's right," he said. "Sam, are you sure about this?"

"It's our only way out," she maintained.

Joe got a firm grip on the middle of the ladder. "Sam, this thing's falling apart. There's no way it can hold any of us."

Boom! They all flinched, dropping the ladder.

104

Lightning had struck just outside one of the barn walls. For a moment they couldn't even hear. The thunder had been like an explosion, leaving their ears ringing. In a dazed voice, David said, "Wow! That was too close!"

"That's it!" Sam yelled. "I'm not going to stay here any longer than I have to. Help me move this ladder and set it up. I'll climb it—I'm the lightest. It'll hold me, and I'm going up there to get us out. Help me!"

"Okay," Joe agreed. The three of them half-carried and half-dragged the heavy old ladder across the floor. They tilted it up. It just reached the loft opening, but the barn was so dark that Sam couldn't be sure it was solidly in place.

"You guys hold the ladder steady," Sam said, her voice shaking a little. "Joe, the first rung is missing. It's the one you pulled loose. Give me a boost."

Joe locked his hands together, Sam stepped on them, and he helped her start up the ladder. As soon as she was on it, he grabbed the rail to hold the rickety thing as steady as possible. Sam climbed up two rungs, and then with a sharp *crack!* the third one broke. Sam shrieked as her foot kicked in the air, but she held on tight.

"Be careful!" Joe yelled. "Maybe you'd better come down."

"No way," Sam said. She hauled herself up, feeling the splintery wood beneath her hands. The ladder creaked. "I'm almost there," she called down.

Then the ladder snapped right in two! David and Joe had to leap back as the whole thing collapsed. "Sam!" David shouted.

Sam had grabbed the edge of the loft, and she was hanging on. She dangled, her legs kicking. "Got to get up," she said. As the boys watched, she slowly, painfully, did a chin-up. She flailed, found a solid board to hold onto, and finally dragged herself all the way into the safety of the loft.

Joe called out, "Are you okay?"

"I'm all right, guys," Sam replied.

The two boys let out a deep sigh of relief.

"Uh-oh, I smell something—smoke!" David yelled.

Sam looked down. The barn wall closest to the lightning strike was glowing with fire. Thick, choking billows of gray smoke were pouring into the barn.

"Sam!" Joe yelled. "The barn's on fire! Hurry!"

The situation has become desperate for my friends! But hang on, guys! Wishbone's coming to the rescue! Just hang in there! And be as brave as Jim Hawkins was when the pirates captured him!

Chapter Thirteen

The next morning a familiar voice called from outside: "Blockhouse, ahoy!" It was Dr. Livesey. Long John rose, put his crutch under his arm, and went outside to meet him. They talked for a moment, and I heard the doctor exclaim in surprise, "Jim? Here?" When the two came inside, I was ashamed to look the doctor in the face, because I felt that in getting myself captured I had failed him. I felt like scolding myself. Bad! Bad! No, no, no!

Dr. Livesey's eyes widened the moment he saw me, but he hid his feelings. He simply nodded to me, then began to treat the sick and wounded. He looked at the man with the bandaged head first and told him he was lucky to have such a hard skull.

Then he asked, "George, how is it with you? You're yellow with jaundice. Did you take your medicine?" And so he worked away, as cool as if he were among friends instead of deadly enemies.

When he finished at last, he nodded again and said, "Well, that does it for today. Now, before I leave, I wish to talk with Jim, please."

George Merry stood at the door, spluttering over some bad-tasting medicine, but he swung around and shouted, "No!"

Long John was sitting on his brandy keg. He slapped it. "Silence!" he roared, and looked around like a lion. "Doctor," he went on, "we thank ye for your kindness, and I think it's right to let ye have your wish. But I'll ask ye, young Jim Hawkins, to give us your word of honor as a young gentleman—for a young gentleman you are, though born poor—not to slip your cable and run away."

I agreed, and Silver rose from his barrel. He told the doctor to climb over the stockade. Then Silver limped across the sandy hill, so close to me that his one leg brushed my fur at every step.

"Go slow, lad," he said softly to me. "The others would shoot us in the back if it looked like we was runnin'." At the stockade fence, where Dr. Livesey already stood waiting on the other side, Silver said, "Doctor, last night the others were ready to slit Jim's throat. The lad will tell ye I saved his life. I'm steerin' close to the wind now, and I'd think it kind of ye if you'd put in a good word for old Long John when the time comes. Remember, it's not only my life now—it's Jim's, too."

Dr. Livesey raised his eyebrows in surprise. "Why, John, you're not afraid, are you?"

Long John looked him square in the eye. "I'm no coward, but when I think of hangin' on the gallows, I get the shakes. But you're a good man and true, and I know ye won't forget the good I've done, no more than you'll forget the bad. Now I'll step aside and let ye and Jim have a word." That said, he limped away, working hard in that loose sand, until he reached a tree stump, where he sat so he could keep one eye on me and the doctor, and the other on the pirates in the blockhouse.

As soon as Long John was too far away to hear, the doctor said sadly, "So, Jim, here you are. You wouldn't have disobeyed and run off if Captain Smollett had been well, but to wait until he was wounded and then desert us—that was cowardly, Jim!"

I wanted to cover my eyes with my paws. "Doctor, don't," I pleaded. "I wasn't deserting—really. And I did a *few* things right. But I was looking for adventure, not running away."

"Jim," the doctor replied sternly, "you had no right to go off on your own, no matter what the reason was."

"I've blamed myself enough. They'll kill me eventually anyway, and I know it. Silver saved my life once, but he can't guard me forever. Never mind that. I can die like a man. What I'm afraid of is that they'll torture me first and learn—"

"Jim," the doctor interrupted, his voice very different, "I can't stand this. Whip through the stockade and we'll run."

Holding my head up high, I said, "No, sir. I gave my word."

"Never mind that. I'll take it all on my own shoulders, holus, bolus, blame and shame, but I can't let you stay here. One jump, and we'll run for it."

I held up my paw to ask for silence. "You wouldn't break your word, nor would the squire or the captain. I won't break mine. Let me finish. If they torture me, I might tell them where the ship is, because I took her and beached her safe and sound in North Inlet." I quickly told him of my sea adventure.

When I finished, the doctor shook his head and said, "Jim, I apologize for ever thinking you would desert us. Every step, it's you who saves our lives. If you hadn't found Ben Gunn, and if I hadn't gone out to talk to him— Silver! Come closer!"

"Aye, Dr. Livesey," Silver said, rising from his tree stump.

When Long John had made his way back, the doctor said, "I'll give you a piece of advice. Put off looking for that treasure as long as you can, and look out for storms when you find it!"

"Tell me what ye mean, sir," Long John said.

The doctor bit his lip. "No. It's not my secret, or I'd tell you. But do your best to save Jim's life, and give me a little time to talk to my friends before you go looking for treasure. Then, when you come to trial, I'll do *my* best to save your neck."

Silver's face was radiant. "Ye couldn't do more, sir, not if ye was my brother."

"Then remember what I said, and if you need help, sing out," the doctor said. "There will be people close enough to give it to you. Good-bye, Jim." He then set off into the woods.

That morning Silver was especially cheerful to the men as they ate breakfast. He told jokes and helped the wounded man eat. All in all, he was more like an actor than a pirate. As I crouched in the corner and gnawed on some salt pork, I saw he was stalling for time, just as the doctor had advised him. But at last the men began to demand that Silver take out the map and lead them to the treasure.

That map—why had the doctor given it to Silver? It didn't make sense! I'd have kept it as safe as my favorite chew toy!

George Merry told Long John to tie me up and leave me in the blockhouse. "No, George," Silver said easily. "Jim's a hostage, and I think it would be better if he came with us. Nobody would dare to shoot at us, for fear of hittin' Jim, ye see. But I'll keep him on a line." Silver slung two muskets over his shoulder, stuck a pistol in each pocket of his coat, hung a cutlass on his belt, and put his parrot, Captain Flint, on his shoulder. Then he tied a line to my neck.

A leash! I HATE leashes! I thought. *An adventurous pup like me is born to run free! And if I HAVE to be on a leash, why does the guy at the other end have to look like something off the cover of* Pirate Monthly *magazine?*

Some of the men carried picks and shovels, others food, but all were armed. We all set out, even the fellow with the bandaged head, and made our way down to the ship's gigs on the beach. The men were in a hurry now, and they never paused, even when I looked longingly at the trees. We climbed into the boats and rowed across the anchorage to the spot marked on the map, which read:

From beach climb hill to tall tree,
S. Point of Spy-glass Hill,
bear a point to N of NE,
Skeleton Island ESE by E, ten feet.

The five pirates were looking ahead and already pointing out trees that were taller than their neighbors. Each one had his favorite. Silver sat in the stern and steered the boat, saying nothing, but at last we pulled ashore again and made our way up the foot of Spy-glass Hill. The eager men ran ahead, but Silver and I walked slowly in the rear. I smelled excitement in the air, and the ground gradually turned springy and soft under my paws. After half a mile, we heard someone shout out from up ahead, and I strained at the leash. "Steady, lad," Silver said quietly to me. "We'll get there soon enough."

When we arrived at our destination, the pirates were standing in a rough circle, staring in horror at something on the ground. It was a human skeleton, stretched out with its arms above the head. "It's a sailor," George Merry said. "Leastways, there's rags of sea cloth still clingin' to his ribs. But why was he laid out like this?"

I stared in horror at the bones. Bones should be decently buried, not left out in the open like this!

Silver looked around. "I think I know," he said. "Here's my compass, and there's the tip of Skeleton Island. Take a bearin' along the line of them bones."

Merry did so. "East southeast by east," he said. "Just like the map says."

Long John smiled. "I thought so. This is a pointer, this skeleton. Thunder! Flint was a cold one. Him and six others came ashore here, and he killed them all. This one he hauled up and laid down by the compass. Flint was always one to protect his money. Shiver my timbers! Six, they were, and six are we, and bones they are now. If Flint was alive, this would be a hot spot for us all."

"He's dead," Morgan said flatly. "I seen him dead in Savannah. Billy Bones took me in to where he lay a-dyin'. But if ever a evil ghost walked, I reckon it'd be Flint's."

"He died hard," another one of the group said. "Ragin' and hollerin' for rum, and a-singin' 'Fifteen Men.'"

I began to get a creepy feeling in my stomach, as if I'd been into a bad batch of kibble. I could smell the pirates' fear strongly now, and it was making me shiver a little myself.

"Well," Silver said, "he's dead now, and the dead don't walk."

We started out again, but this time no one went very fast. Silver no longer had any need to pull my leash tight. I stayed right at his heel the whole time. All of the pirates clustered together as if they were afraid Silver was wrong and that the ghost of the awful Captain Flint was spying on us.

When we came to a spot where the ground leveled out, Silver pointed ahead to the summit of the hill, half a mile off. "There's the three tallest trees over there. We have it now, boys. Do ye want to have a snack afore we starts to dig?"

I perked up, thinking, *Now that you mention it, I could do with a bite—*

"I ain't hungry," Morgan grumbled. "Thinkin' of Flint turned me stomach, like. He were an ugly devil, all blue in the face."

"That was the rum," Merry said. "He drank so much—"

All of a sudden, from the woods in front of us, a high, trembling voice struck up the well-known sea-song:

Fifteen men on the dead man's chest,
Yo-ho-ho, and a bottle of rum!

The five pirates were so astonished that some of them grabbed hold of the others.

"Flint's ghost!" Morgan yelled.

Silver had sat on a fallen log. He struggled to his feet, his face pale. "Quiet!" he commanded. "That's no ghost. It's a voice that comes from flesh and blood, and ye may lay to that!"

The voice in the woods had stopped singing, but now it wailed, "Darby M'Graw! Fetch aft the rum, Darby M'Graw!" It sounded so spooky and unearthly that I whined with dread.

George Merry collapsed to the ground, almost fainting. Morgan was shivering as if he were freezing. "That fixes it! Them was Flint's last words afore he died in Savannah!" Morgan said.

Only Long John remained courageous. "Nobody in this here island ever heard o' Darby, except us. Shipmates, I'm here for treasure, and I won't be beat by man nor devil. I never was feared o' Flint when he was alive, and if that's his ghost, by the powers, I'll face him dead."

Merry was almost crazy with fear. "Belay, John! Don't cross a spirit!"

"Spirit!" Silver echoed with a sneer. "Maybe it was a ghost, but it was never Flint's! It was like him, but it was more like—more like—by the powers, it was like Ben Gunn!"

"So it were!" Morgan cried. "Ben Gunn! Whatever become of old Ben Gunn?"

"Who knows?" said the pirate with a bandaged head, laughing in relief. "You remember what a lunkhead he were. Likely Ben died somewhere, and his ghost come back here to haunt the island. But it's only just Ben Gunn."

George Merry stood up with a smile. "Only Ben Gunn! Nobody minds Ben Gunn, alive or dead!"

I blinked at the buccaneers, surprised at how fast the smell of terror evaporated. Poor Ben. First a washout as a pirate, and now a failure as a ghost!

The pirates were all relieved. Soon we set off, climbing the hill again, with everyone in a better mood. It was steeper as we went higher up, and sometimes I had to crouch low to keep my balance, my stomach fur brushing the grass. When we got to the top, the walking was easier, and the men began to take bearings on three tall trees. The last one fit the numbers on the map, and the men sighted along the line to where the treasure was buried.

By then I had caught some of their excitement. Maybe, I thought, they'd let me dig with them. That would help me get my mind off my troubles, because if there was one thing I loved, it was a good, long job of digging.

The pirates' calculations led them into a waist-high thicket of brush. They plunged in, with Long John and me bringing up the rear again. "Seven hundred thousand pounds in gold, mates!" Merry cried. They all began to cheer, but suddenly they stopped dead.

Silver hunched along on his crutch through the brushy growth, and then he and I halted, too. We were on the edge of a wide, deep hole, like a bowl twelve feet across, not very recently dug, for grass had sprouted on the bottom and the smell of turned earth was old and faint. In the grass were the broken shaft of a pick and the boards of packing cases strewn around and green with mold. On one of the boards I could see the name *Walrus* burned with a hot iron—the name of Flint's ship.

That was all. Someone had dug there, found the money, and taken it. The seven hundred thousand pounds were gone!

Uh-oh! These guys were going to be as unhappy about that big hole as Wanda always is about the tiny little ones I dig in her flowerbeds back home! Speaking of home, when we last left Joe and his friends, they were imprisoned in a burning barn. Like Jim Hawkins, they were in deadly danger.

Chapter Fourteen

Sam could smell the smoke. She hurried through the darkness to the front of the loft. Sure enough, there were big double doors ahead—but they were stuck tight. She kicked them once . . . twice . . . and they finally sprang apart! Gray light flooded into the loft, and in the dimness Sam saw something wedged tightly between two of the wooden beams. She yelled, "Blackbeard's horseshoe! Guys, I found Blackbeard's horseshoe!"

"Can you climb out?" Joe shouted. "The fire's getting worse!"

The fire! Sam looked around, finally finding what she needed. "Here's some rope!" She picked up the sturdy coil and ran back to the edge of the loft. "Grab the end of this!" She tossed down one end of it, and Joe and David seized it. They were all coughing by then, the smoke clogging their lungs. "Hang on tight!" Sam said.

She uncoiled the rope and went back to the open loft door. Would it be long enough? She tossed the other end out the opened doors and down. It came to within four or five feet of the ground. That would have to do!

"Hold on!" she shouted to the boys, coughing. "I'm going to climb down and open the barn door from outside!"

She swung down. She was awfully high up—but it was like the rope in gym class. She let herself down, hand over hand. Overhead, smoke billowed from the opened loft door.

Sam finally reached the end of her rope—literally. She dropped to the ground, sat down hard, then jumped up again at once. Rushing to the barn door, she lifted the heavy wooden latch and swung the door outward. Joe and David spilled out, their eyes red and watering. All three of them stumbled away from the blazing barn, choking and coughing, just as huge flames began to shoot from the opened loft door.

And just then the cavalry arrived! Well, actually, Ellen, Wanda, Mr. Kepler, and I arrived. But we were sure glad to see the three kids! We scurried out of the car and ran toward them!

In the eerie red glow outside the burning barn, Ellen hugged Joe and said, "Are you all right?"

Joe, still trying to catch his breath, nodded.

Wanda stared at the Trumbull barn. It was a mass of flames. "You got out just in time," she said with a sigh of relief.

Mr. Kepler was holding his daughter. "Sam? You okay?"

Gasping, Sam said, "Fine, Dad." To Joe and David, she apologized: "I'm sorry, guys."

Joe laughed. "Sorry? Sam, you saved our lives!"
Wishbone looked up, feeling proud to be Sam's friend. "That's right, Sam! You came to the brink of disaster, but you saved the day!"

Now, if the good guys can only save the day on Treasure Island—or will the pirates win in the end?

Chapter Fifteen

The six men looked as if they had been hit hard. But Silver recovered at once. He passed me a pistol and said with urgency, "Jim, take that, and stand by for trouble!"

The men had plunged into the pit and dug in with their fingers, throwing the boards aside. Morgan found a single gold coin and held it up, cursing. "Two guineas!" he roared. "That's the treasure, is it?"

George Merry yelled, "Mates, there's only two of them, one with only one leg and one nothing but a boy. Cut them down!"

I dropped to my stomach, hugging the ground with my body and forcing my tail to stay down. I hoped that no one would want to hurt the harmless little guy. But I cocked the pistol Long John had handed me, just in case.

George Merry drew a pistol, but just then three musket shots flashed out of the thicket. Merry tumbled down, and then the man with the bandage spun like a top and then fell dead. The other three turned and ran. Merry, wounded in the leg, pushed himself up and pointed his pistol at Silver, but Long John had his own pistol out, and he fired. Merry fell back dead, and Silver said, "George, I reckon I've settled who's cap'n here at last."

At the same moment, the doctor, Gray, and Ben Gunn joined us from among the nutmeg trees. "Forward!" shouted the doctor. "Head them off from the boats!"

"Run, Jim!" Silver urged, taking the hateful leash off. I did run, stretching out all my legs, while Ben Gunn put on the most amazing burst of speed.

Behind me Silver propelled himself as fast as he could with his crutch, his chest heaving with effort and sweat pouring from his beefy face.

When we reached the low plateau where the pirates had paused, Silver cried out from thirty yards behind us, "Dr. Livesey! No hurry, sir! Look there!"

Sure enough, the three surviving pirates were running toward Mizzen-Mast Hill, not toward the boats. I jumped up on a fallen log and watched them flee, feeling like a watchdog who had just chased off three burglars. My friends sat down to breathe, and Long John, mopping his face with a handkerchief, came slowly up to us. "Thank ye kindly, Doctor," he said. "Ye came in the nick o' time to save me and Hawkins. And so it's you, Ben Gunn! Well, you're a nice one, to be sure."

"I'm Ben Gunn, all right," said the strange gray-haired man. "How do ye do, Mr. Silver? Pretty well, thank ye, says you."

Silver smiled in a sad way and shook his head. "Oh, Ben, Ben," he murmured. "To think it's ye who brought me to this."

After resting a few moments, we set out for the boats, and on the way Ben Gunn told us what had happened. It was a story that greatly interested Silver; Ben Gunn, the half-crazy hermit of the island, was the hero of the tale. Wandering the island, Ben had stumbled upon the skeleton and guessed that it served as a pointer. He patiently followed a line from the skeleton until he found a place where someone had dug. He had found the treasure and had carried it on his back a little at a time, day after day, to a cave where he lived. It was clever of Ben—though, of course, I could have nosed out the hiding place myself in less than half the time. Keeping your nose close to the ground does have some advantages.

When the doctor had met the old hermit the day before, Ben had invited all the loyal crewmen to come and stay with him, because he had plenty of food— wild berries and goat meat.

Listening to Gunn, I hoped the doctor and my other friends would be satisfied with the goat meat. I just didn't trust those wild berries!

Ben was afraid the pirates would find him and steal the treasure, and the doctor saw in a moment that it would be better for the loyal men to join Ben in the cave, where they could hold off the pirates. "As for leaving you with the pirates, Jim," the doctor said, "it went against my heart, but I had to do what was best for all of us, and we did think you had run away. I hope you understand."

"I do, Dr. Livesey," I told him, putting my paw on his hand. "If I hadn't run off seeking adventure, they would never have caught me. So after you talked to Silver this morning, you set up an ambush, did you?"

The doctor nodded. "I ran all the way to the cave. I took Gray and Gunn with me, leaving the squire to guard the captain. And we spied you when you stopped to rest. Imitating Flint's voice was Ben's idea. It made the villains pause and gave us time to get to the treasure site before they did."

Silver smiled. "It were fortunate that Jim was with me. If I'd been by myself, you'd have let me be cut to bits and never given it a thought."

"Not a thought," Dr. Livesey agreed in a cheerful voice.

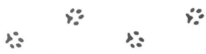

We made it safely to the gigs. The doctor knocked holes in one, and we all got in the other one and rowed for North Inlet, where the schooner lay. It was eight or nine long, hard miles, but Silver, nearly dropping from exhaustion, pulled on his oar without complaining. I sat in the stern and held the tiller in my paws, steering us.

By evening we arrived, all of us worn out. Gray stayed to guard the ship. Then the rest of us climbed up the hill to Ben Gunn's cave, where the squire stood guard with a musket. His face grew red as a boiled lobster when he saw Silver among us.

As soon as we were close enough, the squire called out, "John Silver, you're a prodigious villain! I am told I should not prosecute you because you saved young Jim's life, and I will not. But the dead men hang about your neck like millstones!"

Long John gave him a perfect sea salute and said, "Thank ye kindly, sir."

"I dare you to thank me!" the squire shouted. "Do so again and I'll fight you!"

Silver nodded and remained silent. Inside the cave a big fire blazed, and before it Captain Smollett lay propped up on his elbows smiling at us. But the gold took my breath away. Heaps of gold coins and stacks of gold bars covered half the floor of the cave, shining in the firelight and smelling cold, metallic, and somehow a little evil. That was Flint's treasure that we had come so far to hunt and that had cost the lives of seventeen men from the *Hispaniola.* I began to wonder how much blood Flint had spilled in gathering that gold. Silver could have told me, or old Morgan, or even Ben Gunn, but I no longer had the heart to ask.

"Come in, Jim," the captain said in a weak voice. I crept close to him, almost on my stomach, begging forgiveness. He smiled and patted my head. "You're a good cabin boy in your way, but I don't think I'll go to sea with you again. You love adventure too much to obey your captain's orders!" Then he turned his head. "Is that you, John Silver?"

"Aye, sir, come back to my duty," Silver replied.

The captain just shook his head and said no more.

Oddly enough, John Silver was once again the polite, cheerful cook. He prepared our dinner that night and served it around with a good will, giving me a special bowl filled with tender tidbits of goat meat crowned with a rich gravy. Silver even joined in our laughter. No one looking at him would have known him for a bloody-handed pirate. But I sat close to the doctor, all the same. Silver was a clever man, no doubt, but he was all pretense. The doctor, I realized, was just as brave as Silver, and besides having a good head on his shoulders, he also had a warm heart. I understood clearly just who the better man was.

Yes, sometimes you don't know who your real friends are until you've been through some rough times together. And these times had truly been rough! Rough! Rough! Oh, sorry, didn't mean to bark at you.

The next morning we began to move the treasure down to the beach, a trip of a mile or so, and then out to the *Hispaniola* by boat. We kept a sentry on guard, but the three fellows still on the island didn't trouble us. The work went as fast as we could make it go, but the gold was heavy. I could not even lift one of the bars, so I was put to work packing the coins in bags. That was hard enough for me. After a few hours, I had tasted so much gold that I had lost my appetite for wealth.

So we worked for many days. One evening I heard shouting and shrieking. I called to the doctor, who listened hard and finally heard it, too. "You've got sharp ears, Jim," the doctor said grimly, patting my back. "It's the mutineers. Heaven help them!"

"Don't waste your pity, sir," Silver said. "They're all three drunk, and if they had the courage of a chicken, they'd try to rush us and kill us where we stand."

The doctor looked at him coldly. "Maybe they're drunk," he said. "But maybe they're sick and raving from fever."

"It don't matter either way, to ye or me," Silver replied.

"Well, maybe not to you," the doctor said. "But I swore an oath to treat the sick. Jim, fetch me my doctor's bag."

"You're not going out there alone?" I asked.

"Don't ye do it, Dr. Livesey," Silver warned. "If they don't kill ye, they'll take you prisoner."

"I think I'm safe enough," the doctor returned. Soon he went out alone.

Six hours later Dr. Livesey came back, tired and looking sad. "Fever," he informed us. "Two of them deathly sick with it. I left them all the medicine I could and told them how to take care of themselves. They begged me to bring them aboard, even in chains, but we can't risk it, as few as we are."

That was almost the last we heard of the pirates. We decided that we had to maroon them on the island—to the great delight of Ben Gunn, who said they could live on goat meat for a while and see how they liked it. So we left a good stock of powder and shot, food, medicine, some tools, and some clothes in the cave.

By that evening we had the treasure stowed, along with enough goat meat to see us to the nearest port. At high tide, we cast off the lines and the ship floated free. We anxiously towed her out, rowing in the larger of the two surviving gigs. It was hard rowing, but the schooner came along handsomely, and soon we were all aboard.

The captain still could hardly stand, but he insisted on running the flag up himself. It was the Union Jack, the same one he had flown above the stockade. I felt proud to be an Englishman when I saw it waving bravely in the breeze. With much trouble we set the sails, although some of them were so heavy that when I grabbed the lines in my teeth and pulled, I raised myself off the deck and the sails stayed in place. Silver pitched in and helped me, though I still wouldn't speak to him.

When the sails were up, Silver himself took the tiller and steered us safely to sea. Squire Trelawney called out suddenly, pointing to the island. We gazed out in the distance, and there on the shore stood the three pirates, yelling and waving to us. They wanted to come aboard, but the doctor merely shook his head. "Too dangerous," he said sadly. "We can't risk another mutiny. Anyway, if we took them home, they'd hang for sure. That would be a cruel sort of kindness!"

So we sailed away from Treasure Island.

We were so short of men that we all worked extra hard. Because of his injuries, the captain lay on a mattress in the stern and gave his orders from there. I helped out wherever I could, even taking the tiller now and again, though with all the sails set, it was hard for me to push it with my paws.

We headed for the nearest port in Spanish

America to find new crewmen, and we were all exhausted by the time we reached our destination. It was a beautiful bay, and to the captain's great joy, five British ships lay at anchor in the harbor. He knew the captains of two of them, and he was sure we could put together some kind of crew when they heard his story. The captain, the squire, and Gray went aboard the nearest ship, leaving Ben Gunn and me to guard the schooner.

We should have guarded Long John Silver. He managed to steal a couple of bags of coins. Then, somehow or other, he slipped off the schooner, taking the last of the gigs and rowing away. I saw him leaving and alerted Ben Gunn, but Ben—who was still afraid of Silver—whispered, "Let him go, Jim. He's bad luck, says I. And so he is, says ye, and we're well rid of him. So we are, says I." He scratched the top of my head, which reminded me of the way Silver used to do the same thing.

On thinking it over, I decided that old Ben was right. When the others came back and discovered that Silver had stolen three or four hundred pounds, they were more relieved than angry. He had also left behind his parrot, Captain Flint. I suppose he was afraid she would cry out and give him away as he was leaving. "We're lucky to be rid of him so cheaply," the doctor said. "And bless my soul, but I wish the man well. He's a liar and a thief, but he's got the courage of a lion."

I could not help thinking that if only Long John had been as kind as the doctor, he would have been a very great man. He might have risen to be an admiral in the navy—a top dog.

As the captain had hoped, we got a few new crew members and some supplies aboard—even some grade-A soup bones, which pleased me. We set sail for England within a few days. When we returned, there were only five members of the *Hispaniola*'s original crew left alive, not counting the three marooned pirates and Long John Silver. As the song said, "Drink and the devil had done for the rest."

The treasure we divided fairly, with Ben Gunn getting his full share. As for my mother and me, we had enough to live comfortably for the rest of our lives. Still, for us the Admiral Benbow Inn was home. We used some of the money to repair all the little things that were wrong with it, and Mother bought me a great, soft bed and let me move into one of the old guest rooms, which became my very own. I could lie in the sunlight as it streamed through the window, nibble on a bone, gaze out to sea, and remember my great adventure. Mother and I continued to run the inn, where Long John's parrot now perched near the door and greeted our visitors by calling out strange sailing terms.

I heard nothing more of Silver. He probably found some place comfortable and safe, and with the money he had put by in the bank before the voyage, he may be living as contentedly as we are. I hope so, because he was kind to me in his own way.

According to our map, there are still at least two places on Treasure Island where Flint buried loot, but those treasures can lie there for all time. I wouldn't go back to Treasure Island for gold, silver, prime rib, or anything else. The worst nights I have are when I

dream of the surf crashing around its coasts. And sometimes I sit up in bed, my fur standing on end in horror, with the sharp voice of Captain Flint ringing in my ears: "Pieces of eight! Pieces of eight! Pieces of eight!"

Chapter Sixteen

hat an exciting story! And it had a happy ending, too! Just like real life. Two weeks after the Trumbull barn burned down, Wanda asked David, Joe, Sam, and Ellen over to her house. Mr. Kepler came, too—and so did I, of course.

Wanda announced in her dramatic way, "I've called you all here today for a very special presentation." She held up an odd-shaped package, wrapped in purple tissue. "Samantha," she said, "this is for you."

"What is it?" Sam took the package and tore the paper off. She gasped at what she saw. A plain old iron horseshoe had been nailed to a wood plaque. Burned into the plaque were the words, "To Samantha Kepler, a True Explorer." With her eyes shining, Sam looked up. "It's Blackbeard's horseshoe! How did you find it?"

Wanda smiled. "Well, let's just say someone went through the ashes of the barn and discovered it three days after the fire. It showed up at the historical society, and as president of the society, I decided no one deserved it more than you."

"Thanks," Sam said softly. She looked at her father. "What are you smiling at, Dad?"

Mr. Kepler shrugged. "I shouldn't be. On one hand, I'm disappointed in you. It was foolish to go into that dangerous old barn. But on the other hand, I'm impressed. You showed a lot of courage, Sam. I'm proud of you."

Sam sat beside him on the sofa and gave him a peck on the cheek. "Thanks, Dad. I promise, no more crazy adventures." She looked down at the horseshoe and added softly, "For now, at least."

No one noticed Wishbone. He leaped up on the arm of the sofa and put his paw on Wanda's globe of the world. He gave it a shove, and the globe spun, with strange and exciting places flashing past his nose: Barbados. Hong Kong. Bombay. All places where pirates had once plundered and looted.

Well, Sam, you may be out of the adventure business, but I'm just getting started! This little white dog's got places to go! Sights to see! Trails to blaze! Mountains to conquer! Ahh, I'll do it all—right after lunch!

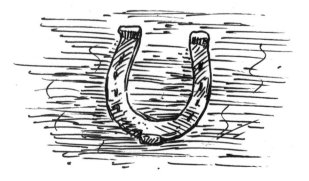

About Robert Louis Stevenson

Whether in pursuit of love, adventure, or better health, Robert Louis Stevenson spent his adult life traveling and writing about the places he visited. Born in Scotland in 1850, Stevenson spent much of his childhood sick in bed with respiratory problems. For entertainment during his illnesses, he and his father imagined stories of robbers and sailors. As a young man, Stevenson devoted himself to writing, and he published many respected travel books and essays. Inspired by a map he drew to amuse his stepson, Stevenson wrote *Treasure Island* (1883), his most famous work. He later wrote the popular *Dr. Jekyll and Mr. Hyde* (1886), and *Kidnapped* (1886). In 1888 he and his family visited a series of tropical islands, hoping that the warm, sunny climate would improve his health. He settled on the Pacific Ocean island of Samoa, where he earned the honorary title of tusitala—"storyteller"—among the natives. He was working on another book when he died suddenly of a stroke in 1894.

About *Treasure Island*

In the fall of 1881, Robert Louis Stevenson found himself stuck indoors through weeks of bad weather. A sickly man, Stevenson did not dare go outside in the cold Scottish autumn rain.

However, he did have some comforts. Like an overgrown boy, Stevenson loved to play toy soldiers with his twelve-year-old stepson, Lloyd. The two happily designed great battles on maps they drew themselves. Then one of their maps took on a life of its own. Stevenson sketched out an island, "in the shape of a fat dragon standing up," as he later described it. He painted in its features with water-colors, and he named it Treasure Island. He told his fascinated stepson tales of the dangerous buccaneers who buried their loot on this lonely patch of earth.

As Stevenson later recalled in an essay entitled "My First Book," he began to see the characters in his mind's eye. He imagined the brave doctor, the staunch squire, the plucky young Jim Hawkins, and the dangerous and tricky Long John Silver. Sitting beside a roaring fire, he began to create chapter titles, and before he knew it, he was writing a tale of high adventure. At first he called his story *The Sea Cook,* but that wasn't exciting enough. Stevenson realized that the book had to be named for the map—*Treasure Island!*

His stepson, Lloyd, helped with plot suggestions, and Stevenson's father, Thomas, also chimed in, all three of them having a wonderful time. Before many weeks had passed, the book was complete. *Treasure Island* first appeared in serial format in a children's magazine beginning in October 1881 (under Stevenson's pen name "Captain George North"), and it was finally published as a book in 1883.

No writer has ever matched this fine tale of life-and-death adventure. Thrilling, frightening, and as fast-paced as a schooner sailing with the wind, it propels the reader along. Like Wishbone, any reader can easily imagine being in Jim Hawkins's place as he fights pirates, searches for hidden treasure, and learns about friendship, honor, and courage. Stevenson wrote about treasure, all right—and his novel is a treasure we all continue to enjoy.

About Brad Strickland

Brad Strickland is a great fan of Robert Louis Stevenson's classic tale *Treasure Island*—and also of Wishbone. He was thrilled to have the chance to write the novelization of the WISHBONE episode *Salty Dog*, one of the plucky pup's greatest adventures.

Brad has written or co-written twenty-three novels, fifteen of them for young readers. One of these works is another WISHBONE tale, *Be a Wolf!*, inspired by the eighth-century English epic poem *Beowulf.* Brad's first novel for young readers was *Dragon's Plunder,* a story of pirates, dragons, and—of course—treasure. With his wife, Barbara, Brad has written stories for the *Star Trek* and *Are You Afraid of the Dark?* book series. He also co-wrote several thrillers with the late John Bellairs.

In everyday life, Brad teaches English at Gainesville College, in Gainesville, Georgia. He loves to go sailing, although he rarely has time to do so. Once, on a short voyage out into the Gulf of Mexico, he even got to steer the *Governor Stone,* a real schooner that was built in 1877. Brad is also an amateur photographer and actor. He and Barbara have two children, Jonathan and Amy, and a whole houseful of pets, including ferrets, a bunny, cats, and two dogs, neither of whom talks—at least not when Brad is listening.